Besotted Bob

Book 13 in The Calendar Girls' Ranch

Kirsten Osbourne

Sign up for instant notification of all of Kirsten's New Releases Text 'BOB' to 42828

And

For a complete list of Kirsten's works head to her website wwww.kirstenandmorganna.com

Chapter One

Marta Martinez took a deep breath, hoping to gain the confidence she needed so badly as she was about to approach the only person, she thought could help her with her situation—Bob Calendar. She glanced into the backseat of her '79 Ford Fairmont and saw that both boys were still sleeping. She debated waking them because she didn't want to leave them alone in the car, but she didn't really want to take the boys along for a discussion this important either.

Her dilemma was over when her older son, Antonio sat up, bumping her son, Mateo, in the process. "Where are we?" Antonio asked, rubbing the sleep from his eyes.

"I'm going to go and talk to a man about a job here. Can you two stay in the car? I'll give you my phone." Marta's phone would be shut off any day now, but for the moment, it worked, and the boys loved to play games on it.

"I'm scared," Antonio said.

Marta nodded, having expected that answer. Antonio tended to be afraid when he didn't know where he was. It would make things a little harder to take the boys along with her, but there was nothing else she could do. "Okay, then. Let me comb your hair." The boys slept in the backseat of the car because there was nowhere else for them to sleep.

She combed their hair and checked her own in a mirror. It desperately needed a cut, and she couldn't cut her own like she did the boys. It helped that she was a woman and could pull it back into a barrette and ignore it.

When she felt like she was as ready as she could be, she took each of the boys by hand and the three of them went to the building Bob Calendar had just disappeared into.

There was one door open, and she stepped into the doorway, smiling at the man sitting there. "Hello. Bob Calendar?" she asked.

Bob nodded, a smile lighting up his face when he saw her boys. "You brought my friends to see me! I didn't think they'd remember my name."

Marta had no idea what he was talking about, but her boys tore away from her and went to Bob. "I don't have my cars in my office." He frowned. "I've got snacks though. Do you boys like beef jerky? I have some cereal with milk as well, but I only keep one bowl and one spoon here in my office."

Antonio looked at his mother, who gave a slight nod. "We can share."

Bob grinned and jumped up to pour a bowl of Crunch Berries for the boys, topping it with milk and adding a spoon. He set the bowl on the corner of his desk, and the boys stood each taking a turn with the spoon. Marta was pleased with how well they were sharing. It would look good on her to have children so well-behaved—at least she hoped it would.

Marta watched the whole exchange with tears in her eyes. He was so good with the boys, but *where* did he know them from? "How do you know my boys, Mr. Calendar?"

Bob frowned at her. "Oh, call me Bob. They didn't tell you? I was sure you were here so they could play. I told them all about my Matchbox car collection and told them to have their parents bring them whenever they could."

She shook her head. "I didn't know they'd ever met you. I'm Marta Martinez, by the way."

"Oh, well I found them at the baseball tournaments in town, and they looked hungry to me, so I bought them each a hot dog." He grinned sheepishly. "I was almost late for my game because I couldn't leave them standing there."

Marta smiled. "Thank you! They wanted to go watch the tournament because their dad had worked for the Royal River Ranch. I'm expecting, and I was just *so* tired. I thought they would be all right in a crowd because they are good at screaming." Even Mateo with his speech impediment could scream like nobody's business. She wasn't sure if that was a skill or not, but she couldn't complain. The boys were safer that way as far as she was concerned.

Bob laughed. "They seemed just fine, and I'm sure everyone thought their parents were right there. We don't have much crime in Cauldron Valley."

She frowned. The crime that had been there had all been because of her husband. "May I sit, Mr. Calendar?"

"Bob," he corrected again.

"Bob," she repeated. "I need a job. My husband was killed a few weeks ago, and I need to be able to support my boys. I was a housekeeper for the hotel in town, but they fired me when some information came out about my husband."

He nodded, and she could tell he understood—everything she had and hadn't said. "You don't have the same hobbies your late husband did, do you?"

Marta blushed and shook her head. "No, I don't." Unfortunately, she understood what *he* hadn't said as well. "I know this is a long shot, but I need a job to be able to feed my children."

"You were a housekeeper?"

She nodded. "I was."

"Then you can clean this building we're sitting in every day around six and keep up with the cabins as the kids check out. And I'll need an hour a day from you for cleaning the bathrooms in the cabins. Will that work?"

Closing her eyes for a moment, she nodded, feeling extremely relieved. "When can I start?"

He shrugged. "Tomorrow?" She looked much too tired to start immediately. He turned on his computer and quickly tapped on the employee program, glad he could give her a job. It had become too much for his mother and Brunie to clean the cabins, so this was working out well as far as he was concerned. His mother could still do the work, but she was too involved with her grandchildren to care that there was work to be done. "Full name?"

"Marte Martinez. My friends call me Marta."

"Doesn't Marte mean Tuesday?"

"Yes, it does."

He nodded, spelling her full name out to her to be certain it was spelled correctly. "I'll make a note that you prefer Marta." After tapping a few keys, he asked, "Address?"

Marta blushed, not wanting to answer, so she was sarcastic instead, "Only thing I can give you for that is my license plate number."

Understanding dawned on Bob's face, but Marta refused to look down. It was her truth, but with his help, she hoped it wouldn't be for long.

"I would offer you a cabin, but we don't have extras right now. We had to build more for this summer." Bob was obviously deep in thought for a moment. "Let me see if I can pull some strings. I'll be back in a minute."

Marta stayed where she was seated, staring at her boys, who were happily reaching the end of the bowl of Crunch Berries. She hadn't been able to splurge on sugary cereals, needing something that would fill them up for cheaper. How she was living now wouldn't bother her nearly as much as it did, if it wasn't for the boys. Her boys...they deserved better than she did.

When Bob came back a short while later, he smiled at her. "All right, I have a place for you. You'll have room and board as long as you're working for the Calendars. When the fall comes, you and the boys are welcome to move into a cabin, or you can stay in the house. It doesn't matter to us either way."

Marta blinked at him a few times. "Stay in the house?"

He nodded. "I don't have an apartment I can put you up in, but all of my sisters but one have moved out, so Mom and Dad have extra rooms. Mom said they'd love it if you took two of them for you and the boys. Dawn and Todd have one, and they'll still have two spares. I guess you could even have three rooms if the boys want their own space."

"Your parents are going to allow the wife of the man who sent someone to rob them to move into their home? Do they know who I am?" Marta was stunned that he'd offer her a place in his family's home. She was sure she didn't look like a dangerous criminal, but it was pretty clear she'd been married to one.

"They do. And Mom said she'd love it if the boys just called her Grandma." He looked back at his computer. "So, let's finish getting you into the system, and I'll take you to the house and show you your new rooms. You'll have a private bath, and the boys will have a bath to share. That work?"

"I...I don't even know what to say!"

He shrugged, grinning at her. "I have a soft spot for the boys," he said softly. Glancing at them, he could see the boys had finished their meal. "Are you two still hungry? Or is it time to let Mom and the baby eat?"

Antonio looked like he was torn. He looked at his mother, and then he looked at the bowl. "I'm still hungry, but Mom and baby can eat first."

She shook her head without hesitation. "You and your brother eat. Mom and baby are fine." She had eaten a quick snack in the car to combat her plummeting blood sugar. Marta had always experienced low blood sugar during her pregnancies.

Antonio smiled happily. "More for us! Thank you, Mr. Bob!"

Marta was pleased to see her sons remember their manners with their "friend." Everything was going so much better than she'd imagined it could.

After the boys were settled with another bowl of cereal, she gave him the information he needed for her employment records. "You'll have health benefits," he said, planning to pay for those with his own income. He couldn't ask the ranch to pay for something that was unusual. They already paid for health benefits for his aunt Brunie, so it wasn't fair to ask them to pay for another person. Everyone but family was considered seasonal. "And meals are served at the house at six, noon, and six thirty. Snacks are available any time. Mom will watch the boys when you have to leave to work. Do you have any questions for me?"

Marta's jaw dropped as she gaped at him in shock. "You haven't even checked my references..."

He shrugged. "I know your boys. They're polite, and they are thankful. I don't need to know more than that. I'm sure your husband didn't raise them to be that way. It was all you. So, I know what kind of person you are, based on them." He smiled at the boys as they ate the last few bites of the cereal. "Do you guys want to go meet Grandma? She's going to be watching you while your mama works!" Something occurred to him then, and he frowned. He hadn't been around pregnant women until the past few months, and those were his sisters. "Is it going to be too hard for you to clean?"

She smiled, shaking her head. "Not at all. It sounds like it will only be a few hours most days."

"The only days that will be hard are Saturday and Sunday. We have our camp 'graduation ceremony' on Saturdays around noon, and the new campers are here Sundays around three. You'll have to clean all thirty cabins in a little over twenty-four hours. I'm sure if you need help, I can get someone to help though."

She nodded, realizing it would be a big job, but at four months along, she should be fine to get it done during the summer. "And summer is the only time you have the overnight campers, right?"

"I think we're going to do a 'Winterfest' weekend starting this year, but there will be no hurry getting the cabins cleaned, because we won't use them again until June."

She nodded. "I'll be pretty big by December, which is when I assume Winterfest will happen. I'm due on Christmas Day."

He smiled. "Wait until March to clean then. It won't matter. The only thing that you'll need to do during the off-season is the office here, and the little buildings, but most of my sisters are good at cleaning their own areas." His mother was going to be thrilled to have the cleaning off her plate. "All right, let's go to the house, and I'll show you your new home and introduce you to my mom."

Marta bit her lip. "Are you sure she doesn't mind?"

He laughed. "Mind? She's thrilled. She wants all her grandkids living here with her, but none of my sisters will agree, so she's adopting your two as grandkids. I keep my old toys in the house for my nephews, so your boys are going to have plenty to play with, and they will not be lacking love." Bob got to his feet and waited for Marta to follow suit. He glanced at the bowl, seeing it was empty again. The boys must not have had much to eat recently, because they'd even drunk the milk that was left at the bottom of the bowl.

He led them along the sidewalk—which was slated for Todd to grow flowers on as soon as he finished the vegetable garden Mom had requested—to the main house. He opened the door, calling out loudly, "We're home!"

Dawn popped out of the living room, wearing her dirtiest clothes. "Hi!" she said, her sightless eyes staring straight ahead. Obviously, she'd been helping Todd with the gardens before the kids arrived that day. She was liking gardening almost as much as she loved her new husband.

Bob smiled. "This is my sister Dawn. She's the only one who still lives at home, and her husband Todd lives here as well."

Marta looked at the girl, and immediately knew she was the blind sister she'd heard about. "It's nice to meet you, Dawn," Marta said softly.

"You too!"

Bob looked at Dawn, knowing his mother had already filled his sister in on the new arrangements but filling her in for Marta's sake. "Marta and her boys will be staying with us. The older one is Antonio, and the younger is Mateo. They're going to be staying in two of the rooms our sisters vacated."

"Sounds good to me. I miss the noise that was always in the house. I sure hope you boys make a lot of noise!"

Marta laughed. "You'll get your wish there."

Mom walked down the stairs then and she smiled at Marta. "You must be Marta. I'm Beth, and I'm so excited to have you here." She looked at the boys. "I'd love it if you called me Grandma!"

Antonio smiled at her. "Okay."

"Let me show you your rooms."

Marta was thrilled that Beth was so openly happy to have them there. She glanced at Bob who didn't seem surprised by anything. This family really was as special as she'd been told.

Beth led them up the stairs, and into a room where there were three beds. "We can all just share this room," Marta said, thrilled there was a place for them.

Beth shook her head. "There's no need," she said. "There's another empty room just like it next door. A woman wants her own space. You do not need to be sharing with your boys. There's plenty of room here."

"But what if your grandchildren want to come stay? There needs to be room for them!"

Beth laughed. "We'll still have two spare rooms for them. Don't worry about that at all. Besides, they're kids. They'll pull out sleeping bags and have a slumber party if there are no beds."

Marta smiled, knowing Beth was right. "All right then. I'd love to have some privacy."

"You boys are staying in here from now on," Beth said. "Do you like it?"

Antonio and Mateo both nodded. It was bigger than the room they'd had in their apartment.

"Now, come with me. Mom's room will be next door, but you need to see where it is." Beth led them to a room right beside the one the boys were in. "This will be Mom's room." Marta was surprised when Beth led them down the hall. "And this is my room. If you get scared at night you can go to Mom or to me. Okay?"

"Okay!" Antonio said, speaking for both of them as usual. Mateo stuttered, so he didn't usually try to speak in front of people.

Marta couldn't believe how quickly and easily they'd been accepted—both as employees and as boarders. She'd made the right decision when she'd come to Bob Calendar for help. Thank God.

Chapter Two

Bob helped Marta get their things from her car and carry them up the stairs. "I can do it all," he said as they made their first trip. "You probably shouldn't be doing so much in your condition."

She laughed. "I'm in my fourth month. I worked until I went into labor with both boys. I don't need to even worry about that."

"If it gets too hard, you just let me know."

"I'll be fine."

"I'm going to give you half of your first week's pay in advance," he told her as they dropped suitcases off in her room. She'd sold all her furniture for money for gas, a used car, and food. She'd expected it to stretch more than it had, but nothing seemed to work well for her.

"You don't have to do that." Then she thought about the phone in her pocket that would be shut off any minute, but she couldn't let herself worry about the phone. Who was going to call her anyway? Everyone she knew had abandoned her when the news came out.

He shook his head. "You need to have money for gas or if you want to take the boys out for ice cream." He tilted his head to one side. "How would you feel if I took the boys for ice cream? I promise I'm not a creep, I just really enjoy children."

Marta looked at him for a moment and then nodded. "I think that would be all right." She didn't get any bad vibes off Bob, which made her feel good about him. She had from Luis...but her father had said he was a good man, and she should marry him.

"Good. I'm getting another load of stuff and then I can show the boys the toys in the family room." He hurried off down the stairs, and Marta couldn't help but wonder how the man had remained single for so long. He was attractive—too attractive for her tastes—loved kids and was genuinely giving. He should have been married years ago.

She followed down the stairs at a much more sedate pace. She'd fallen downstairs during a pregnancy with a child who would have been between Antonio and Mateo and lost the baby within a few hours. She mourned for that baby every day—more than she was mourning for Luis. Of course, as soon as Luis had died, she'd found out a great many things about him that made her realize she'd never known him to begin with. It was strange how very lost she felt, knowing she'd devoted the last seven years of her life to a man who she had never even really known.

When she reached the car, she saw that Bob was handing the last of her things to Antonio to carry up the stairs, then he'd picked up a big black bag which had all their dirty clothes in it. She hadn't felt that she could waste the little money they'd had on laundry. She'd even considered going down to the river and washing it as they had on the Oregon Trail.

"Nothing more for me?" she asked, thinking that she could use the money he gave her to head to a laundromat. She wouldn't have a uniform for this job as she had for the hotel, so she would need those clean clothes soon. All of her maternity clothes were in that bag. She was wearing a pair of stretchy waist shorts, and a shirt that was three sizes too big. Maternity clothes weren't exactly attractive, but they were better than what she was wearing.

Mrs. Calendar approached her, and she saw that Mateo was following her with a cookie in his hand. "In my house, everyone does their own laundry. I taught my girls to wash as soon as they turned ten. I'll show you the washer and dryer, and you're welcome to use it whenever you need."

Marta couldn't believe how very kind this entire family was. "Thank you, Mrs. Calendar. I can go to a laundromat if that's easier on you."

"Not at all. I tend to do all my laundry on Mondays, so choose a different day. And we still have two washers and dryers because it was hard with all the girls living here, though I miss them more than I can say."

Surprised, Marta asked, "Don't they all come every day to help with the children?"

"All but Junie, but it's not the same as knowing they were sleeping just down the hall. I know it's strange, but I'm used to always having them around."

Approaching the washers and dryers, Mrs. Calendar showed Marta the special features on them, and showed her where she hung clothes as they came out of the dryer. "I'm a much better housekeeper than I am a cook. I hate to cook."

Marta smiled. "I enjoy cooking on occasion. Cooking for my children day after day becomes difficult." She'd never really cooked for Luis much, because he'd always been hanging out with his friends in the bars around town. He wasn't there until well past the boys' bedtime, and then he was just there to sleep and have sex. "I can take over cooking a couple nights a week if that would help."

Mrs. Calendar laughed. "Berry cooks for us every day still. She's married now, but she teaches cooking to the children."

"And you really don't mind if my boys and I join your family for meals? They don't have the best manners..."

"Of course, they don't! They're little boys. No one is expecting anything from them. I promise."

Before Mrs. Calendar wandered off, Marta took her arm. "Thank you for your hospitality, Mrs. Calendar. You have no idea what it means to my boys and me."

"Please, call me Beth. I'm just tickled pink I could help you."

As Beth walked away, Marta felt tears popping into her eyes. She'd hoped for a job and perhaps a small cabin for her and the boys, but this? She was overwhelmed by the generosity of these people. Who would allow a stranger to live with them? But more than that, who would allow a stranger who had been married to a man intent on robbing them to live with them?

Within seconds the tears turned into full-blown sobs. Marta wasn't sure if it was the relief of having a place to stay or her hormones getting the best of her or what, but it didn't really matter. What mattered was getting somewhere private so she wouldn't be caught crying like a crazy woman when she hadn't even been there for a day.

She dashed through the house as quickly as she could, straight up to her room. Just as she was about to open her bedroom door, a hand reached out to her, touching her shoulder. "Are you all right?" Bob. It was Bob.

She nodded but didn't turn to him, determined to hide the tears. He slowly turned her and took her into his arms, holding her close. It didn't take Marta long to collapse against him. Within a minute or two, the shoulder of his shirt was sopping wet, and she pulled away. "I got your shirt all wet," she said, sniffling.

Instead of retreating, Bob shifted her to his other shoulder. "That's okay. There are still dry spots."

Marta couldn't help but laugh. "How do you always know the right thing to do?"

He shrugged. "Good parenting, I guess."

She pulled back and looked up at him, her deep brown eyes still shining from the tears she'd shed. "Thank you, Bob. Thank you so much for everything you've already done for my boys and me. I don't think I could ever express just how much it has meant to me."

He smiled slightly. "Lunch is in twenty minutes. My sisters are all out eating with the campers, but Mom, Dad, Brunie, and Melvin will be there, and so will I."

"I can't believe someone takes the time to make lunch for the family."

"Don't expect anything fancy. Lunches during camp days are simple. Probably soup and sandwiches. That's what Berry and her class usually make. She'll add a nice salad and some fruit, and you'll feel like you've feasted."

"Has anyone let her know there are three extra people to feed today?"

"Trust me, she knows." Bob smiled. "You okay now?"

Marta nodded. "I've just been running on nerves for so long with having to deal with the boys on my own, and not knowing where I was going to get the money to feed them... I feel like I have time to melt down and cry now, if that makes sense. Of course, being pregnant doesn't help any of that."

He smiled, glancing down at her baby bump. "I think you're adorably pregnant."

She laughed. "With this being my fourth pregnancy, I feel like I'm huge. I wasn't this big until my seventh month with Antonio!"

"Four pregnancies?" he asked. Had she given up a baby for adoption?

"I lost a baby between Antonio and Mateo. I fell down the stairs at work." As much as she mourned that baby still, she was able to talk about it easier than she had before. Besides, Bob was so sympathetic, she felt like she could talk to him about anything.

"I'm so sorry!" He knew his mother had lost a baby before him, and she still got a faraway look when she mentioned that lost baby. It had to be so hard to lose a child.

She smiled. "Thank you. I'm going to go and wash up before lunch. I need to put a cold rag on my eyes, so I don't look like I've been crying for hours."

"No one minds," he said automatically. "You're free to express feelings in this house."

She gave a half-laugh. "That's silly. My husband never allowed me to mourn that baby. He told me that God took her, and I didn't need a girl anyway." Luis had been kind at times, but mostly the man had been an ass. If she'd believed in divorce, she'd have left him long ago. But she'd been raised to stay with her husband no matter what, and so she had.

"He was wrong." Bob stroked her face with the back of his finger. "I think you need to be around people who know how to treat you for a while."

She smiled because she had no other answer to that. It felt strange to already be so familiar with this man that he was holding her as she cried and caressing her cheek. But she liked it. Way more than she should. "I'll be down in a few minutes. I think the boys are both in their room putting their clothes away." She'd have to do it again later, but it made the boys feel good to have a place to put their things. There were a few toys she'd brought, but not much had fit into her car. She just prayed these people continued to be kind to her and the boys. Everyone could be kind for a day. Ongoing kindness? That seemed to be much harder for people.

She washed her face and was pleased that it wasn't as blotchy as she'd expected. This family was...much more than she'd imagined, and much better than she deserved. She was pleased they were there for the boys though.

She stopped into the boys' room as soon as she freshened up. "Are you boys ready for lunch?"

They looked at her with wide eyes. "We had cereal and cookies already!" Antonio said, looking amazed.

"And now we get lunch." Marta smiled at how excited the boys looked to have real meals for a change. They'd mostly snacked before, nuking ramen in gas stations, so they could eat. But they had to hide what they were doing, and she'd always felt so guilty for it.

Mateo clapped his hands. "I...I...want to stay!"

Marta laughed. "We're going to, mijo. I promise!" *At least until they realize we're not worthy of their kindness and kick us out.* She'd have to start saving money immediately for that eventuality.

As they went down the stairs and joined the family in the dining room, she wasn't sure at first where to sit, and then she saw that someone had placed a booster seat in one of the chairs. Mateo didn't hesitate as he climbed into it, so she sat down beside him and put Antonio on her other side.

"Is there anything I can do to help?" she asked, after getting the boys settled.

A girl with real curves walked into the room then. "Not at all," she replied. "I'm Berry, and my girls will serve lunch. We have it all ready."

"Your girls?" Marta asked. She didn't look old enough to have girls who could serve a meal.

"The girls I teach in the summer. This is a new cooking class, so they aren't making anything complicated, but what they make is still wonderful." Berry sat down in a chair near the kitchen, and then looked around, noting who was there. "Girls!"

Six girls carried in plates with sandwiches and fruit all dished up. Each sandwich had a little skewer with a cherry tomato through it. A small bowl of mac and cheese was set in front of Marta for the boys.

Beth smiled. "If the boys would prefer to go to camp, they could do that instead of staying with me."

Marta looked at the boys. Antonio nodded excitedly, but Mateo shook his head. "Would it be all right if Antonio joined the camp, but Mateo stayed with you?"

"Absolutely!" Beth said, her eyes on the little boy. "We're going to have fun together."

Mateo smiled. "C...c...cars?" he asked.

Bob nodded enthusiastically. "I put my cars up in the family room. Will Andy come and play as well?" he asked, referring to his sister Julia's younger son.

Beth shook her head. "No, sadly all of my grandchildren will be at camp this summer. Only Mateo will play with me, but I'm thankful for Mateo."

Marta just listened as everyone talked around her. A large salad was brought out, and she took a bowl. It felt strange to eat something healthy after weeks of eating in the car.

The boys took the mac and cheese happily, and they ate their sandwiches. Someone had gone to the trouble of making the boys grilled cheese instead of the BLTs the adults had.

Marta's eyes met Berry's. "Thank you for doing extra for my boys."

Berry grinned. "It was no trouble at all. I love to cook."

"That's obvious."

"She has a trophy that proves she's the best cook in all of Idaho, Wyoming, and Montana," Beth said with a smile. "I'm proud of her."

"You should be." Marta took a big bite of the salad and said a silent prayer of thanks that her baby would have good nourishing meals—at least for a little while. It made her feel like she wasn't a failure at being a parent.

Chapter Three

Bob walked over to the house that evening, excited to eat supper with the family and their new guests. Marta wasn't going to start working until the next day, which still worried him, because he didn't think she should work on so little sleep. Who could sleep in a car anyway?

He couldn't believe how drawn he was to the woman. She was pregnant, for gosh sake! He shouldn't be lusting after a pregnant woman, but he told himself it was better than lusting after a married, pregnant woman. What attracted him so much was that she wasn't trying to blame anyone for the situation she found herself in. She admitted right away who her husband was, and he'd known why she was left destitute immediately.

He knew that after Luis Martinez had been shot and killed in a shootout with the police, his bank accounts had been seized immediately. Bob wished he'd taken the time to look into the situation a little bit more, but at the time, his sister was marrying his new best friend—her husband, who had come to rob their house, Todd.

When he got to the house, Todd was there talking to Dawn and Marta, who was listening to the conversation even as she tried to make sure her boys weren't running around the house like maniacs. He could see the motherly look in her eyes as they shot everywhere the boys went. The same look had been in his mother's eyes for most of his life. She still watched his sisters and him as if they were children.

He walked to the three of them and smiled down at Marta. "Dawn, how did music go today?"

"Wonderful! I walked into the music room and heard one of the male campers playing the piano. I probably should have been there early, but April was looking for Santa outfits online for all the babies coming this winter, and no matter how many times I nudged her, she wouldn't stop until the outfits were ordered." Dawn sighed dramatically. "I did however discover that one of my new music students plays piano brilliantly. I asked him if he'd had lessons, and he just shrugged, saying he'd found a music book and 'figured it out.' I was so excited!"

"That's great! Maybe you can nab him and ask him to be part of the carolers for the Christmas Village. I don't know if he can sing as well, but even if he can't, you could sing and not be stuck behind the piano," Bob suggested. Though they'd met their fundraising goal for this summer's programs, they were already starting to raise money for next year. There was never enough to offer scholarships to all the kids who deserved them.

"He can sing, *and* he plays piano! The kid is a marvel."

"I'm sure he doesn't hold a candle to his teacher," Todd said softly.

Dawn blushed and leaned into her husband. "Maybe in your mind."

Bob rolled his eyes at Marta. "All of my sisters are newlyweds, but Dawn is the newest of all the newly marrieds. Sometimes the love fests get a bit overwhelming."

Marta smiled. "The first year of marriage is the hardest, but also the best," she said softly. Luis had changed as soon as she'd gotten pregnant, which was just a couple of months into their marriage. He'd started staying out later and going to bars with his friends after work instead of going home. She was sure he was afraid of being a father at the time, but now she wasn't quite so certain. Since then, he'd only seemed to need her around when he was ready for sex. The rest of the time, he pretty much ignored her.

"Dinner!" Beth called from the dining room, and Marta turned. There were lots more people there for supper than there had been for lunch.

She saw that the same chair had a booster seat in it, so she and the boys headed that way. Mateo was all smiles, but he wasn't talking around the strangers, and who could blame him? His own father had been disgusted by his stammer. It broke her heart to see him feeling so lost, but here...everyone seemed to accept him here. Hopefully that wouldn't change when he started talking in front of them. She'd known the Calendars for twelve hours, and she wanted to never leave.

Mr. Calendar, who had been introduced as Bert, said a prayer as they sat down, and to Marta's surprise, he thanked God for bringing her and the boys into their lives. How could this family possibly be so forgiving? She'd half expected them to put a padlock on the outside of her door to lock her in at night. They didn't even seem wary around her.

The meal was a simple one, but there were little daisies made out of pineapples and grapes on each plate. Potato salad, baked chicken, and salad was the main meal, but there was a plate of hot dogs for the boys. Someone was looking out for her boys, and she was thrilled. With as little as they'd eaten lately, she felt thrilled that there was food they'd eat.

Beth started the conversation. "What did you do before you came to us?" she asked.

"I was a maid for the hotel in town. Most of the time I was the only maid, so I was worked way more than I should have been, but the boys were allowed to go to work with me if they sat quietly while I cleaned, so I never complained." Marta smiled at Mateo, who had sat quietly coloring every day while his brother was in school, and Marta worked.

"It sounds like it was a good arrangement. We'll do our best to do the same here, but the boys won't need to go with you because I'll be able to watch them when they're not at camp."

"I think I'll mostly be working in the mid-mornings and in the evenings. I hope they won't get in your way."

Bert shook his head. "Not at all. My wife wants one-hundred-sixty-nine grandchildren. It'll be easier for me if we can borrow two...or three as the case may be."

Marta smiled. They were already talking about the baby after it was born. She felt like she was in a dream, but she resisted the urge to pinch herself to wake herself up. No, this was a dream she'd keep wrapped around her as she slept in her car and did her best to feed her children.

"I'm happy to share my children. Thank you so much for all you've done for us."

Bert shook his head. "No need for thanks. We're happy you're here."

The food was wonderful and after the meal, Marta got to her feet. "I'm going to go and get started working, if that's all right with you, Mrs. Calendar."

"Beth...but Bob said you needed sleep. You may not work tonight."

Marta bit her lip. "But how will I pay you back for your generosity then?"

"There's no need. But I wouldn't mind if you would be the one to do the dishes tonight. We have an industrial strength dishwasher, so we don't even have to rinse the dishes well, but I hate loading it so much!" Beth shrugged. "I'm just not too terribly domestic."

Marta smiled. "I'd be happy to do the dishes. That sounds like a good compromise." She was truly relieved, because she had to do something to help, but she was so tired, she knew it couldn't be much. And she was going to be able to bathe the boys that night for the first time in a good long while, she would have clean children. She couldn't wait!

She went into the kitchen where everyone brought her their plate. Bob gathered the boys' plates for her and stayed in the kitchen as she worked on the dishes, talking to her about their operation. "If you're up for it," he said, "I'd love to take you on a walk to show it to you when the dishes are done."

Marta thought about how very tired she was, but with everything Bob had done for her and her family, she had to be willing to at least go for a walk. "I'd love that." Besides, it would be good for the boys to be out in the sunshine. Lately she'd been going to parks and letting the boys play while she napped a little bit in the car. This baby was weighing on her more heavily than the others had. Of course, she hadn't been homeless with her other pregnancies.

She finished up the dishes and started the machine, walking into the living room to find the boys on the floor, playing with some cars they'd found somewhere.

"Okay, boys, we're going for a walk. Are your socks and shoes on?" Marta asked.

Antonio frowned. "I want to keep playing with cars with Mateo."

Mateo didn't say anything, but his huge eyes filled with tears.

Beth smiled at Marta. "I'm going to keep the boys while you walk. There's no need to drag them out when they're content where they are."

Marta shook her head. "I can't ask you to do that."

"They're my new honorary grandsons. It's a privilege."

"I don't want to take advantage of your kindness."

"You're not! I'm begging to spend time with them." Beth smiled at Marta. "Let Bert and I play grandparents, and you go for your walk."

"Bob just wants to show me around."

Beth's eyes sparkled. "You two have fun!"

Marta worried for a moment that Beth saw her as a prospective wife for Bob, but then she dismissed the idea. There was no way the woman would consider Marta good enough for her only son. She had two children, was pregnant with the third, and her late husband had...well, she didn't want to go into that even in her thoughts.

Bob led the way, opening the door for her, and nodding for her to go through ahead of him. "This ranch was settled in the mid-1850s by Calendars who made the long walk along the Oregon Trail. We still use the original cabin as an outbuilding. The area was settled by four prominent families, and those families are still all here today. They were the Calendars, the Cauldrons, the Larsons, and the Royals."

She nodded. "Luis worked for the Royals, and I knew they had history in the area, but I moved here after I was married when Luis got his first job. I was eighteen and fresh out of school. Blind to his faults."

Bob nodded. "I hope you know no one here will blame you for anything he did."

"I would," she said softly, embarrassed about the direction their conversation had taken, but she wasn't about to deny all that had happened.

He shook his head, taking her arm. "There's a small step here. About six inches wide. A big step and you'll be over it."

Marta looked at Bob. "I can see it."

He sighed. "I'm usually with Dawn when I walk the grounds. Sorry." But he wasn't. He'd taken the opportunity to touch her, and he wasn't letting her arm go anytime soon. "My grandfather decided to turn this place into a girls' ranch. We still have a few cattle we run, but they're mostly just to show the girls how to rope and ride if they have that desire. My sister Val is in charge of the equestrian aspects of the ranch."

"It's been a girls' ranch for that long?" she asked, surprised.

"It has. We started with just overnight camps over the summer, and when Dad first took over, he extended it to include day camps, where kids could come and learn different things, they were interested in but still sleep at home every night. When I took over, I added in afterschool camps and Saturdays, so we were running year-round. Just last year, we voted as a family to add boys into our girls' camps. So now we're the Calendar Girls' and Boys' Ranch." He grinned. "Todd is our new baseball coach. We have soccer, baseball, football, and basketball for the boys, but girls can get involved in any of that as well. And the boys are welcome to take Berry's baking class or one of the craft classes. There are several boys who spend time in the library, ride, and take the music classes. I think there's only one signed up for cooking with Berry, but hopefully that number will grow."

"Am I right that you have twelve sisters all named after months? That's what I heard, but I need confirmation on a rumor like that."

Bob laughed. "I do. I am my mother's only biological child. When the doctor told her she couldn't have more children, she decided she wanted the perfect number of children—lucky thirteen, so she adopted twelve daughters and named each after one of the months, so they would be Calendars."

"And do you call them by their month names? I noticed Dawn isn't a month."

He smiled. "Dawn's full name is December. She got the last month of the year because she's the youngest. Mom and Dad adopted them all in batches. January, February and March were the first year, and then April, May and June the next year. In four years, they adopted twelve girls. January goes by Jana. She works with autistic kids. She got married in October, and they're adopting a little girl they'd both been working with from the foster care system."

"Oh, that's lovely! Is she autistic?"

"Very high functioning, but yes, she is. She was kicked around a lot by the system before Jana took her in. Then February goes by Val, short for Valentine. She's the horse fiend around here. Then March goes by Marci. Marci teaches science."

"Do kids really want to learn science in their free time?" she asked. It would have been the absolute last thing she'd have chosen to do, but children were different all over.

"You wouldn't believe how busy her classes always are. She takes the kids out to find critters, and she explains each little thing. I sure wouldn't have taken it, but the kids love her. Then April just goes by April. She's our Christmas addict. The girl cannot wait for Christmas, and she starts planning for the next Christmas on Boxing Day."

Marta found herself relaxing with him, thrilled he was telling her so much about his family. "She sounds like fun."

"Oh, she is. Exasperating at times, but who isn't? May is the quietest of the whole bunch of us. She's an animal lover and a reader. She runs our library here on the ranch, and she provides critters for Jana and Marci on a regular basis."

"Does June go by June?" she asked. With their names being so different, she was sure April, May, and June were thankful for more "normal" names.

"She actually goes by Junie. She is the only one who has a job outside of the ranch, and she does the books. She was the first to move away from home."

"Do you live here on the ranch?" Marta asked.

Bob nodded, stretching his arm out to point. "That's my cabin there. I needed my own space, but I need to be close to home as well." He glanced down at her in the fading light. She was so pretty. "Next comes Julia. She's our resident artist, and she teaches art classes to anyone and everyone. She even has an adult class in town. Then August is Sparky. She loves computers and gadgets and everything to do with them. She's also an amateur ghost hunter, but don't tell her I said amateur."

Marta smiled, nodding. "And next is?"

"Berry. Short for September. She cooks, as you've seen. She makes supper every night before she returns to her husband on Larson Ranch. Then comes October. She uses her full name. We tried different nicknames with her, but she never liked them, so everyone just calls her October. October named November Novel. Novel is a writer, and she lives for situations where she can watch people and take notes on their behavior. And you've met Dawn, our musical prodigy."

"I'm never going to keep them straight! Are any of them related by blood?" she asked.

"Not to my parents and me, but April, May, and Junie are triplets." When she didn't lick her fingers and raise them to the sky, Bob grinned at her. "They're going to love you!"

"Why?"

"Because you don't think triplets are unlucky like the rest of Cauldron Valley."

She rolled her eyes. "This is a very strange town. You know that don't you?"

He laughed. "I do. I think that's why I love it so much."

Chapter Four

After showing her around the ranch, Bob led her down the walk to the river, where he and his sisters had often gone during the summers with all their friends. "There's a rock we can sit on overlooking the Royal River. The sun is about to set, and it will be the most beautiful sunset you've ever seen."

Marta smiled, shaking her head. "I'm letting your mother take care of my sons for a sunset?" It didn't seem right. She'd had no time for fun in her life since she'd had Antonio. Her husband had only been at home at night, and he told her repeatedly they couldn't afford a babysitter, so she'd taken care of children and worked. Many times, doing both at the same time. She'd worked seven days a week, and he'd never even watched the boys when he was off on the weekends while she worked.

He chuckled. "I promise, she doesn't mind. She's looking at the two of us and already seeing you in a long flowing dress and veil."

Marta shook her head. "No, she's not. She's trying to figure out how she can make you see that I'm as unsuitable as a woman comes."

"Why would you think that?" he asked.

She sighed. "Look at me. I'm four months along with my third child. My sons are three and six, and the little one stutters. My husband died *in a shootout with the police*, and I've been living with my children in a car for the past month. Why would your mom even consider me as an option for you? I'm no prize."

"Because my mother sees people, not their pasts. She sees you as a genuinely good person who cares for your sons so much you would do anything for them. It's written on your face every time you look at them."

"Being a good mother, doesn't make me a good daughter-in-law prospect."

Bob laughed at that. "You don't know my mother at all if you say that. The most important thing in my future bride will be that she is a good mother. Nothing more nothing less. Mom wants all of us married, and she wants us married yesterday. Now that my sisters have all tied the knot, she's looking at me to do it next."

Marta smiled. "Your mother is very sweet, but I'm sure she's looking for a woman who has never been married to a criminal and doesn't bring two children into your life."

"My mother cares about nothing that happened to you before you set foot on this ranch. If we walked back into the house now and I said we were getting married, she'd start planning the wedding, no questions asked."

"You are *loco en la cabeza*!"

He chuckled. "Not even ashamed of it. I'll make you a bet..."

She turned to him, grinning a little, realizing they'd made it to the river. He sat down on a rock and took her hand, pulling her down as well. "What bet?"

"We go back to the house, and I tell my mother I'm marrying you. If she gets excited and starts planning the wedding, then I win, and you have to marry me. If she doesn't like the idea, I'll give you a thousand dollars." He had the money in his account. He rarely spent anything. His sisters always loved to talk about how cheap he was, and he didn't deny it. But if he was married to this magnificent woman, who was doing so much for her children, he would feel free to spend. He'd want to pamper her and the boys.

"That's a crazy idea," she said, her faint accent coming through in her voice. Having been raised in Texas and not Mexico, she had always spoken English as well as Spanish.

"But if you're that sure she wouldn't accept you, why not? Don't tell me you couldn't use the money."

She took a deep breath. His mother had surprised her so far, but Marta was certain she'd say no to them marrying. "I could use the money. But you know nothing about me."

"Then tell me about you."

She smiled. "I grew up in a small Texas town. I was an honor student and determined to go to college and possibly law school. I liked the idea of helping immigrants become legalized citizens of the US, and there's a lot of need for that in the part of Texas where I grew up. My senior year in high school, a man caught my attention. He worked for one of the ranchers outside of town, and I thought he was handsome. My friend and I saw him in the store one day, and she dared me to say hello. His name was Luis Martinez, and he was the cowboy I had always dreamed of marrying."

Bob looked at her and nodded. "Go on." He knew where her story was going of course, but he was curious as to how she would tell it.

"My parents were determined I would graduate from high school before I even had a boyfriend, so I couldn't date him. But as soon as I graduated, he went to my father and asked for my hand in marriage. We'd spent very little time together, but he was so handsome, and I'd been dreaming of marrying a cowboy for years...My father said yes, and I married him three days later. Right after we married, he found a job working for the Royals, and we came here, and I said goodbye to everyone I knew. At first, I thought about going to college online, but Luis didn't like that idea. I come from a big family like you. There are seven children, and I was the oldest. I think my father was glad I was off his hands, but Mama cried a lot when I had to leave." She sighed. "I called them when Luis died, and asked if we could come back to Texas, but Papa said it wasn't a good idea. I would have to figure things out, but since it was the best way to grow up, he knew I could do it."

"What about his parents?" Bob couldn't imagine turning a child away like that. His parents' door would stay open to every one of their children and any stray who came along. It was just how they were.

"I never met them. They're from Mexico, and he was raised there. I sometimes wonder if he married me just so he would be able to get his citizenship easier. I was born and raised in Texas, and my mother as well. My father's family came to the US when he was just five, so he barely remembers Mexico." She said the name of the country the way her parents had, with an H sound instead of the X.

He shook his head. "Well, it sounds to me like you need someone to help you through all this. You could marry me."

She shook her head, laughing. He was keeping his silly gag going much longer than she'd thought he would. "That would be silly. Not for me, but for you. It would be very smart of me to agree and saddle you with two boys and another baby on the way. But why would you want that?"

Bob wasn't sure how to answer. "When I first saw you this morning, even before I looked at the boys, I thought to myself that you were the woman I needed to marry. My aunt Griselda claims she can see if two people are meant to marry, and my mother says she got the ability from her aunt. Now, I don't know if it's true, but I could see in Mom's eyes she wants us to marry."

"That cannot be true!"

Bob pointed off in the distance as the sky shone a fiery pinkish blue as the sun slowly sank behind the mountains off in the distance. "Watch."

As she watched the sun set, Marta felt something come over her. She had no idea what it was, but suddenly she was at peace, sitting there beside a man she barely knew, but had heard so many wonderful things about. She rested her head on his shoulder, sighing contentedly. "That is the most beautiful sunset that I have ever seen." She'd seldom had time to watch sunsets, but she was glad she'd taken the time for it that day. She would never forget it.

Bob turned toward her, using his index finger to lift her face, and he slowly lowered his lips to hers. It was a soft tentative kiss, and she found she was more moved by it than she had been by anything she'd ever done with Luis.

She turned to him more fully, wrapping her arms around Bob and hanging on for dear life. What she was doing must be wrong...she'd only lost Luis six weeks before, but it felt...it felt so right.

When he lifted his head again, Bob gazed into her beautiful brown eyes. "Marry me, Marta."

She laughed. "If your mama likes the idea, then yes, I will. But don't get your hopes up." She felt like she was living in a fairy story where everything she needed or wanted came true. How could she say no? She'd be waking up in a few hours with a crick in her neck from trying to sleep in the car anyway.

He leaned down and kissed her once more. "Let's go tell everyone!"

"I have to get the boys ready for bed anyway," she said. "They both need a bath before they can sleep on clean sheets."

He shrugged. "They're boys. They don't care."

"No, they don't. But *I* do." She'd gotten a shower while the boys napped that afternoon, and it had been the most glorious thing. She was finally clean after living in her car for so long.

Marta got to her feet, more exhausted than she'd been in a long while, but she had a night of sleep ahead of her. In a real bed, unless she was dreaming, of course, in which case, she'd wake up in her car.

He took her hand and headed toward the house. He knew his mother would be walking on air. She was like that.

As they walked, he told her that his family never did long engagements. "Two days sound good?" he asked.

She sputtered. "Two days?" It wasn't like she had anything she was supposed to be doing, even if it wasn't a dream. "Sure, why not?" It was Thursday. A Saturday wedding sounded good. "I definitely don't need a white dress anyway."

"Of course you do. I can't wait to see you walking down the aisle toward me."

She laughed. "I'm going to be really disappointed when I wake up in my car and realize this was all just a dream."

Instead of pinching her, Bob kissed her, his hand stroking up and down on her back. "You're not dreaming," he whispered against her lips, "unless I am too. And I sure hope I'm not."

When they got back to the house, she told the boys it was time for a bath, but Beth smiled. "They already had baths, and I put them in some pajamas I keep around for just such an emergency."

Marta was so tired she hadn't even noticed. "Thank you so much, Beth. I'm dead on my feet."

"I noticed that this morning, and you haven't slowed down all day." Beth looked back and forth between the two of them. "Bob, do you have something to tell me?"

"Marta just agreed to marry me," Bob said, his smile lighting up the room.

Neither of his parents looked surprised, but his mother looked absolutely delighted. "Let's go try your dress on. Bob, put the boys to bed."

"My dress?" Marta had never felt more confused in her life. "What dress?"

"The one I made for Bob's bride."

Marta's hand rested on her belly. "I'm sure it won't fit."

"I'm sure it will." Beth clapped her hands, so excited. "Saturday sound good for the wedding?" she asked Bob.

"Sure," he said, grinning at the look of utter confusion on Marta's face. "I'll put the boys down. I think I need to tell them a bedtime story anyway. A story about two young princes who are about to get the father they need."

Bob obviously wasn't worried about his ability to parent, Marta thought. It was the first flaw she'd seen in the man—overconfidence. Parenting was the hardest thing she'd ever done. It couldn't come easily to anyone...even Bob.

Beth had her hand and pulled her up the stairs toward the master bedroom. "Come with me."

Marta was pretty sure she didn't have a choice, so she followed Beth into her room, noting how clean everything looked until she really looked and saw the clutter everywhere. There seemed to be a hundred craft projects in various stages of completion.

Beth disappeared into her closet and came out holding up a pure white wedding dress. "Where did this come from?" Marta asked. It looked like it was let out in the waist.

"I made it for Bob's bride years ago when I made dresses for my girls—all except for my girl who wouldn't have worn one anyway." Beth held it up in front of Marta and squealed. "It's perfect for you. The bodice is simple, but the dress flares out at the hips, and it will hide your belly a little. Not that your belly bothers me one whit. I'm excited to have a new grandbaby." Beth pushed the dress into Marta's hands. "Go try it on."

Marta took the dress and carried it into the adjoining bathroom obediently. As she undressed, she wondered what on earth she'd gotten into. She was marrying a man she'd met that morning, and his mother had made her a dress—that would fit over her pregnant belly—years before? Was she really dreaming, or had she slipped into the *Twilight Zone*?

The dress fit her like a glove, all except in the belly area, where it flowed out and flattered her baby bump. How had the woman known to make a dress for a pregnant woman years before? It made no sense, but it fit...and it suited her. She hadn't had a real wedding dress the first time, and she'd been disappointed that she didn't. She'd married in a pink dress her mother had made for her graduation.

Now, here she was marrying a stranger who was better to her than she'd dreamed a man could be, and she was handed a wedding dress that fit her perfectly. That had been made before the seamstress had known she existed.

She stepped out into the bedroom and showed Beth the dress. The woman walked in a circle around here, tugging at the dress here and there. "I don't think I need to do anything to it. It fits perfectly!" Beth stepped toward her and wrapped her arms around Marta. "Welcome to the family!"

"I...I'm not good enough to marry Bob," Marta blurted out without even realizing the words were coming.

Beth smiled, taking Marta's hand in hers and walking to the bed to sit on the edge. "That's why you *are* good enough for him. Because you don't *think* you are, so you'll be a good wife to him trying to be good enough. See?"

"Not really."

"Trust me." Beth's hand went to Marta's baby bump, stroking it. "When do you find out the gender?"

Marta laughed. "My mother always told me that only a fortune teller can see the future, and that's what finding out the gender of the baby makes you—a fortune teller. So, I will find out around Christmas when this baby is born."

Beth sighed. "I'd like to know, but I'll love the baby either way."

And Marta no longer worried that Beth Calendar thought she wasn't good enough for her son...though she wasn't sure if believing it was in her future.

Chapter Five

When Marta woke the next morning, she blinked several times, trying for a moment to remember where she was, and then it all came rushing back to her. She was safe in the Calendar house, and the boys were sleeping in the next room over, and not in the backseat.

She got up to empty her bladder and brushed her teeth, dressed, and headed to the boys' room. She opened the door a bit to make certain she didn't wake them, but both were gone. She pulled her phone out of her pocket and checked the time again. It was seven-thirty. She hadn't slept more than three or four hours at a time in a good long while because if her pregnant bladder didn't wake her, the boys did.

She walked down the stairs, wondering what sort of mischief the boys were in, and found them with Beth, who was trying suits on them in the middle of the living room. "Good morning, Marta! I'm trying to see if I have suits that will fit the boys. We haven't spent a dime on any of the twelve weddings that have taken place in our family in the past year, and I'm determined to keep that streak going, if only to keep my husband quiet. He keeps complaining about how much the weddings cost." She rolled her eyes.

Marta could hear the even sounds of excited screams coming from outside, and there was a gathering of boys in baseball clothing that she could see out the window behind Beth and her boys. "How have you managed twelve weddings with no out of pocket costs?" That sounded impossible to her.

Beth shrugged. "I've had all the dresses made for years, and I even made bridesmaid dresses. Do me a favor and tell all the girls you love the bridesmaid dresses and ask them to wear them. It'll be fun to see their faces."

"I...I haven't even met your daughters." How was she supposed to tell them to do something if she hadn't met them yet? That was craziness.

"They're all going to poke their heads into the cabins while they're off today. You've met Dawn and Berry. The others will come by and meet you as well. Not Junie, because she's working in town today, but you'll meet her Saturday."

"Where is this wedding happening?" Marta asked. Her first had been at the courthouse in Texas, but she really wanted a church wedding this time.

"Oh, at the church in town. I'm assuming you went to the church in Mountain Home. I hope you won't mind going to the church here in Cauldron Valley."

Marta shook her head. "I had to work on Sundays, so I never got to go to church." Luis had even insisted that she trade in all her time off for cash, so she'd worked every day until she'd delivered her babies, but she'd gone back to work just days after each of the boys was born.

"Well, that's just sad. You'll love our church, and you shouldn't have to work on Sundays. I think we're going to hire an assistant for you. Brunie and I are too old to get the work done, and you're too pregnant. We'll have someone else do the floors."

"But...that's why I came here. So, I could work." Marta couldn't imagine not doing the job she was paid for when she'd only been there a day.

Beth nodded. "And you're staying here so you can marry Bob and be a member of our family. I'll tell Bob we need to run an ad."

"I would feel bad if you did that."

"Well, you're not working on your wedding weekend, so someone is going to have to fill in for you. I'm sure we can find someone who could use the extra cash." Beth seemed determined never to return to her job of cleaning cabins.

"I need to go out and work on cleaning now." Marta needed something to eat first, but if she'd slept past breakfast, she wasn't sure if it was okay.

"Breakfast first! You need to keep my grandbaby healthy." Beth nodded toward the kitchen. "We put a plate of waffles and bacon into the microwave for you. Just heat it up for a minute and it'll be ready." She poked Mateo in the tummy, and he giggled. "Right, Mateo?"

Mateo nodded, his hair flopping everywhere as he did. Antonio jumped up. "I'll sit with you while you eat, Mama."

Marta was surprised. Antonio never left his little brother with anyone else. He must really trust Beth or really want to talk to her. Maybe both. "Sounds nice."

She walked into the kitchen and pushed the buttons on the microwave to cook her breakfast. Someone had left some syrup on the counter for her to use. She opened the fridge and got herself a glass of milk to go with the food, and carried it all to the table, where Antonio was waiting for her. "How did you sleep?" she asked.

Antonio smiled. "It was nice to sleep in a real bed again."

Marta smiled. "I'm sure it was. Did Mateo get scared?"

"He didn't. He always used to climb in my bed with me, but he slept in his own bed last night."

Mateo had always been afraid of his father. The man was so gruff with him, demanding he speak properly. She was certain he felt more comfortable in the new house. "I'm glad."

"Me too. He kicks!" Antonio shook his head. "Mr. Bob had breakfast with us, and he said we could call him Dad now, but I don't *want* to call him that."

Marta felt a pang in her heart. Antonio had just lost his father, and she was asking him to call a new man by his father's name. "That's all right. You can keep calling him Mr. Bob."

"No, I want to call him *Daddy*. Remember when Dad said I was too old to call him Daddy and I had to call him Dad? I didn't care, but Bob feels like a daddy to me."

"I'm sure Bob would be pleased if you called him Daddy."

"He would?" Antonio asked. "I was kind of afraid to ask…"

"I don't think you need to be afraid to ask Bob anything at all. He cares for you boys a great deal." Marta took a bite of her breakfast, wondering about living arrangements. She and her boys had just moved into the house, and they were comfortable. She had no idea how large Bob's place was, though he had pointed in its direction as they'd walked the night before.

Berry walked into the house then, leading a gaggle of girls. They went straight to the kitchen, and Marta wished she had time to just sit and listen, but she needed to start work. She was a decent cook, but from what she'd heard about Berry, there were lots of things Marta could learn from the family's cook.

Antonio smiled. "Mateo said good morning to Bob this morning," he whispered.

"He did?" Marta's eyes widened in surprise. "He never talks around people he doesn't know."

"I know! He was excited to talk to Bob, though. I could tell. He stuttered even more than usual."

Worried about Bob's reaction to her son, she closed her eyes. "What did Bob say?"

"He said good morning back, and then he put Mateo on his shoulder and carried him to breakfast." Antonio shrugged like it was something that happened every day.

Marta smiled. She'd made a good choice with Bob. She didn't love the man, but she knew she could. Hopefully, he could love her back and not just her boys. She was certain most second marriages started differently, with the man loving the woman, and not her children. Thankfully, Bob wasn't like most men.

After she finished eating, she asked Beth where the cleaning supplies she needed were.

"Oh, they're in the same building where Bob works. You should go say good morning to him anyway. He did a good job with the boys this morning."

"I shouldn't have slept so late," Marta said, shaking her head. "I was just so tired."

"Of course, you were. You moved here yesterday. You should get a few days of sleep." Beth looked at her for a moment. "You're sleeping in tomorrow as well. The bathrooms won't need to be done, and I've rallied my daughters to do your cabin cleaning so you can enjoy your wedding."

"But that's not fair to them!" Marta protested.

"As Jana put it, 'It'll be nice to have a new sister.' No one begrudges you anything. I'll tell you about my family someday, and how we came to be." Beth smiled. "They'll all work together, with the pregnant ones on lighter duty, so it will be an easy job."

Marta frowned. "Bob told me."

"Bob doesn't know everything." Beth smiled. "Run along and clean. I have some important playing to do!"

Marta laughed. "I'll be back for lunch!"

"We'll see you then."

Hurrying to the office building where Bob worked, she slipped in the side door and went to his office. He was on the phone, but he grinned when he saw her, holding up one finger to indicate she should wait.

She stood in his doorway and watched him talk to whomever was on the other end of the line. "Thank you for understanding, and we appreciate the discount." He smiled. "The kids will be excited. I'll talk to you next week."

Bob leaned back in his chair and motioned for her to come toward him with one finger.

Marta laughed and walked in, wondering what he was up to. The look on his face when he'd first seen her had told her he didn't want to call their engagement off, which would have been her worry otherwise. "Good morning. Thank you for seeing to my boys and letting me sleep."

He took her hand and pulled her down onto his lap. "Our boys, and we need to keep Mama healthy so the boys can be healthy." He nuzzled the side of her neck. "I think the boys are going to keep calling me Bob if you don't mind."

She pulled away and looked at him. "Why do you say that?"

He shrugged, looking sad for a moment. "When I told them this morning they could call me Dad, I could see on Antonio's face that he didn't want to do it. I'm not sure why, but he hated the idea. I'm sure it's because he just lost his father. I can understand that."

She smiled, stroking his cheek. It felt strange to be as comfortable as she was with a man she'd met just the day before, but they were engaged, which was why she should *really* feel uncomfortable, but she didn't. "Antonio's father told him to start calling him Dad and not Daddy because it was time for him to become a man. Antonio wants to call you Daddy. He thinks you're a daddy and not a mean dad."

Bob blinked a couple of times, and then a slow smile spread across his face. "Nothing would make me happier."

"I thought you'd be fine with that. Antonio sat with me while I ate breakfast so he could tell me what he wanted. He just wasn't sure how you'd feel about it."

"I'm all for him calling me Daddy. Love the idea." Bob looked downright excited to be a daddy to her boys. The man was like Mary Poppins—practically perfect in every way.

"I do too," Marta said. "I need to get off you. I'm too heavy to be sitting on your lap."

Bob chuckled. "Don't you dare! I like you right where you are." He tightened his arms around her and sighed. "Mom is trying to figure out something, so you won't have to clean this weekend, but she and Brunie are definitely retired."

"She has your sisters pitching in. It's solved."

"Well, that's good news. Did you like the wedding dress Mom made? You don't have to wear it, but it would make her really happy if you did."

Marta nodded emphatically. "I love it. I think it's really weird that she made a wedding dress for your potential bride that was sized for a pregnant woman, but I'm afraid to ask too many questions about that."

Bob laughed. "Mom is special like that. You'll see."

They talked for a moment about the plans being made, and then Marta stood up. "I need to get to work. That's what I'm paid for."

"It is!" He grinned. "If you need anything, just call me."

"I don't even have your number! We're crazy!"

"We're not." He had already programed her number into his phone. He tapped her name and hers rang. "There, you have my number." He watched as she answered and then hung up, adding his number to her phone. "You know...we should get your number onto my cell phone account. There's no need for you to even have to think about paying that bill."

"I can continue to pay my phone bill."

He shook his head. "Nope. You and the boys are moving in with me tomorrow, and I plan to pay the bills. You could quit your job if you wanted, but you may want to have your own money."

Luis had always had an account separate from the one her paychecks went into. She paid all the bills, and she never knew what happened with his money. When she found out he'd bought some land for a hide-out for his gang, she wasn't pleased. Of course, by the time she'd found out, he was already dead, and the world was falling apart around her.

"I think we should share an account, if that's all right with you," Marta said. She'd feel safer if he didn't have secret money. She trusted Bob, but she'd once trusted Luis as well.

"That sounds wonderful. That's how I think married couples should be."

"Maybe you'll take some time to show me your house this evening."

He nodded. "I'd be happy to!"

As she wandered off to clean her first bathroom, Marta wondered how on earth she'd found such a wonderful man. She was still waiting to wake up.

Chapter Six

Marta got all the bathrooms cleaned in about two hours—including sweeping up a mess of sand in one of the boys' cabins. Each cabin was two huge rooms with bunkbeds and a bathroom in between. It was much easier than the work she was used to doing at the hotel.

Many different women popped their heads in at different times. "You must be Marta!" an extremely pregnant woman with a huge grin said. She was tiny, dressed in jeans, and had a dark tan. "I'm Val. February, if that helps you at all."

"So good to meet you, Val. When are you due?" Marta was thrilled to see she wasn't the only pregnant woman around so some of the focus would be off her.

"October." Val rubbed her obvious baby bump. "I need to get back to the horses. I just jumped over here to see you during the break between classes."

"I'm glad you did!" Marta thought for a moment about what Beth had told her to say. "I'm supposed to tell everyone to wear their bridesmaid dress tomorrow."

Val groaned. "I totally forgot about those hideous dresses. We have to wear them?"

"That's what Beth said."

"One more time if it'll make her happy, but then we get to have a bonfire and burn them."

Marta laughed. "That bad?"

"Worse!" Val raised her hand in a wave and hurried away.

A few minutes later a woman in jeans, t-shirt, and toolbelt popped in. "I'm October, and you're Marta. You're pretty, and I can see why

Bob adores you." There was a young girl about a foot behind her. "This is your new niece, Lacey. She's pretty amazing."

"Hello, Lacey. Hi October." Marta saw that both were dressed the same, with identical toolbelts. "It's good to meet you both. My sons are at the house."

"We'll meet them at lunch today then. We eat with the family when we feel like it, and today, we feel like it."

Marta smiled. "Sounds good. I wish you'd *all* eat there, so I could meet everyone at once."

"We all try to eat at the house on Sunday after church. There's no way all of us could eat together for lunch during the summer. We take turns with the kids as they have their lunches."

"You serve meals to all of them?"

October shook her head. "I teach a class in carpentry that only a few girls are willing to take. I have more this year because boys. There's a mess hall where the overnight campers eat, but most of the day campers just bring their own lunches."

"What if they don't bring a lunch?" Marta asked, feeling badly for the children whose parents couldn't afford lunches.

"Berry and her first class of the day make up lunches for all the kids who forgot theirs or whose parents don't provide them." October sighed. "We have enough scholarshiped kids that we sometimes have to provide lunches for twenty or so kids per day. Berry and the girls whip them out, and then those kids can just grab a bagged lunch as they go to the lunch tent."

"I think it's great you guys feed so many." Marta had heard so many things about this family, and it looked to her as if they were all true. Much of the rumors had seemed like tall tales that were much too good to be true.

October smiled. "It's part of the service we provide."

After they were gone, Marta wondered for a moment where she would fit into this wonderful family. She would keep cleaning, but there had to be more places. She just hoped she could find one that suited her.

Another sister came in a few minutes later, and she looked just as pregnant as poor Val had. "I'm Marta," she said.

The girl hugged her. "I'm Jana, the oldest of the months." She was of mixed race and wore shorts and a sleeveless maternity top, her hair in a bow atop her head. "This is my daughter, Aubrey." Aubrey looked to be African American.

"It's nice to meet you both. Bob mentioned you to me last night." Marta didn't add that he'd given her a quick rundown of all the sisters.

"Well, it's nice to meet you. So excited you're marrying Bob. *Someone* has to!"

Marta laughed. "You're not a Bob-fan?"

"Oh, we're all Bob-fans. He's one of the best men around, but he's a pain in his sisters' backsides. I hope you're not having a girl, because that man...he's going to be the one to meet the boyfriends at the door with a running chainsaw."

"Oh my!" Marta could see it though. Bob already loved her boys so much. What if he had a daughter of his own?

Jana laughed. "And rumor has it we're all wearing ugly bridesmaid dresses again?" she asked, wrinkling her nose.

"Beth asked me to have you wear them."

Jana sighed dramatically. "Then I guess we're wearing them. I'm glad she made the flared waists or some of us would no longer fit in them."

Another sister stepped in then, at least Marta assumed it was a sister because all the women on this ranch seemed to be sisters. It was overwhelming. This one was Asian, and Marta realized that her being Hispanic wouldn't bother these people at all. They were already a mix of different races.

Jana looked at the sister. "This is March or Marci, as we all call her."

Marta smiled. "It's nice to meet you, and I'm glad I'm getting months. It helps to keep you all straight."

Marci wrinkled her nose. "I guess."

"You're the one who teaches science, right?" Marta couldn't help but wonder who was with the children as everyone met her.

Marci nodded. "Bob is watching over classes for a few minutes each so we can meet you. I have a free period right now, but he's with Jana's class, and they need her back, so he sent me to find her."

Jana's eyes widened. "What happened?" She obviously wanted to be prepared as she went back to the children.

"Billy is having a meltdown," Marci said. "He hates it when you leave."

Jana nodded, took Aubrey's hand, and the two of them hurried back to class.

"She has all the autistic kids as her core group, and she doesn't get to take any breaks all day. She's with the kids."

"I understand," Marta said. "I think her job may be the toughest."

"And the most rewarding," Marci said. "Jana loves those kids so much, and so many of them who start out with her full-time, get to move on and be in the other classes. And that's where she found her daughter."

Marta nodded, wondering if maybe she could help Jana when there was time. "It does sound rewarding."

"Oh, trust me, it is." Marci smiled. "I'm on lunch duty today, so I'm going to go and get some lunch from Berry and then get back to it."

"Have fun."

"Oh, summers are the best around here! So much fun!"

Marta finished the bathroom she was working on and moved on before another sister could stop her. As she was pulling her cleaning cart to the next cabin—thank God there were sidewalks—a girl in a green t-shirt that said, "Is it Christmas *yet?*" walked up to her.

"You must be April!" Marta said, grinning at the girl. "I love your shirt."

April laughed. "Welcome to the family. Yes, I'm April, and you need to be part of the live nativity scene we're doing this year. When are you due?"

"Christmas Day."

"Oh, good. You should be able to hold out most of the month then. Maybe you'll go late, and the nativity will be preserved a little longer."

"I'm not so sure about that." Marta shook her head. "I tend to go early."

"Well, try not to this time, okay? Can you keep your legs crossed?"

Marta laughed. "I don't think that would work."

"We'll see. I believe in Christmas miracles!" April grinned. "Okay, Dawn said I could leave for just a minute or two while she taught, but she needs me back. There's one kid who feels the need to throw stuff if I'm not in the room to watch him. He thinks it's fun to have a blind teacher. Eventually the boys will have the same respect for Dawn that the girls do." With that, she ran off toward another building, and Marta continued pulling her cart along the sidewalk.

Marta walked past a building where there were computers everywhere, and she had to wonder if it was Sparky's classroom or Novel's. Or did they share?

Someone came hurrying out of the building toward her. "Hi! I'm Novel and you're my new sister." Novel grabbed her in a hug. "Okay, have to get back to work. I hate that dress, but I'll wear it for you. Not for Bob. Only you! See ya!" Before Marta could say a single word, the girl was back inside.

Marta wasn't sure what to think of Novel, but she'd reserve her opinion for a time when they could sit and talk. She passed another building that looked like a library and stopped there for a moment to watch someone who looked a great deal like April read a story to the children there. She searched her mind for a moment, but she couldn't for the life of her figure out which sister it was. *It must be May or Junie, but I can't remember which is the librarian and which works somewhere else. I'll ask Bob.*

She didn't run into any more Calendar sisters before finishing the cleaning for the morning, and she returned the cleaning supplies to the closet in the main office building, and Bob called to her as she was putting the mop and broom in it. "Wait for me. It's just about lunch time, so I figured we'd walk over there together."

Marta smiled. "Sounds good to me."

When Bob joined her, she said, "I met most of our sisters today. I saw Jana, Val, Marci, April, either May or Junie was in the library, but I can't remember which. Berry was in the kitchen, and I met October and Novel. I guess I still need to meet May, June, and Sparky. The rest I've at least spoken to."

"And? Did you like them?" Bob asked, his hand taking hers as they walked toward the main house.

"I did! Novel was a little whirlwind, and I'm not sure how I feel about her, but I'll know more when we have a chance to sit down together. Your mom said she wants them wearing their bridesmaid dresses, and none of them seem to like that idea. One of them—I can't remember which, because they were all a blur—said that we'd have a bonfire and burn all the dresses after the wedding."

Bob laughed. "They hate them, and they all had to wear them for every wedding. My dad is super cheap—I get it from him—but he would have had a fit if Mom had done different bridesmaid dresses for each wedding, so she made twelve of them, and said the girls had to wear them for every wedding. Thankfully, October eloped, so they only have to wear them eleven times each."

"Wow." Marta grinned. "Your mom is...something else. I'm still baffled at how she had a dress waiting for me. But it's perfect."

"Yup, that's how Mom is." He opened the door of the main house for her, and she walked in, going straight to the living room to find the boys racing cars while Beth sat on the couch, knitting needles clicking madly.

"Hi guys! How was your morning with Grandma?" Marta felt strange calling someone that to the boys, but they both smiled at her.

Mateo ran to her and threw his arms around her. "It was f...f...fun. We p...p...played with c...c...cars!"

Marta wasn't sure her younger son had ever spoken so much at once, and especially not in front of anyone but her and Antonio. "I'm so glad. Did you get a snack?" she asked.

"C...c...cookies."

Antonio came up behind his brother, his grin huge. "Aunt Berry made cookies with one of her classes, and we got to taste them to make sure they were good enough to give everyone for lunch!"

Marta grinned, her eyes meeting Bob's, who was standing behind her to one side, his hand on her shoulder. "I think that sounds like it was a wonderful morning. I'm glad you had fun," Bob said.

"It was fun, Daddy," Antonio said, watching Bob to see his reaction to the new name.

Bob squatted down so he was on level with both boys. "I'm glad you want to call me Daddy. It makes my heart so happy it wants to burst."

Antonio threw his arms around Bob and held tight, and Marta stood watching them with tears in her eyes. "Me too," Antonio said, and Mateo got in on the hug, but was silent.

Beth met Marta's eyes, and she saw the older woman had tears as well. She needed to sit down and have a long talk with her future mother-in-law, and she hoped it could happen soon after lunch while the boys napped. Antonio always fussed about napping, but he did better when he could take one.

Bob looked up at Marta and smiled, and she saw there were tears in his eyes as well.

Marta didn't know what she'd done to deserve a man like Bob who loved her children with everything inside him, but she wished she knew so she could do it again. Her boys were happy with this man.

Chapter Seven

Lunch was hectic that day. The sisters who hadn't yet met Marta all tried to pop in and at least say hi to her—all except Junie who was working in town, which meant it was May in the library with the kids. Marta felt overwhelmed, and she was thankful she needed to help her boys with their meals. It helped her be just a bit less nervous as she met her future sisters-in-law.

Bob sat on the other side of Mateo from her, and they took turns getting him more food. There were too many people there for him to talk, so he would nudge one of them and point at what he wanted. Marta hoped that Mateo would feel comfortable with this big, boisterous family soon.

The food was delicious as always, and the raspberry lemonade cookies with white chocolate chips were to die for. The boys each took two more, and Marta decided not to worry about what they ate that day. They were refilling their batteries after a good long while of having little to eat.

Bob was as caring and attentive to the boys as she was, and she couldn't be happier about it.

"How can I help this afternoon?" Marta asked.

Beth shook her head. "You can rest up for your wedding tomorrow."

Marta frowned. "I don't need to sleep nonstop. I got a solid eight hours last night, and I haven't slept that much in...well, since before the boys were born." Luis had considered the children hers to deal with. He only came in and made his opinions known when there was something he didn't like.

"That's my point!" Beth said. "You're going to have a new baby soon, and then you'll never get to sleep. If you sleep now, while help is available, it would be better for you and the baby."

Marta sighed. "If I rest that much, I might just lose my mind."

Bob chuckled. "Why don't I show you my cabin today, and you can think about how you want to rearrange things and even start to move things in."

The word cabin made his house sound tiny, but she didn't let that deter her at all. She and Luis had shared a two-bedroom apartment with the boys. They could easily make a bedroom and just a living room work. Her boys loved sleeping on the floor. "That would be wonderful if you can take the time."

"It's our busy season, but I can take a little. I need to pay attention to my fiancée, don't I?"

After the meal, she put the boys down for their nap, telling Bob she'd meet him in his office when she was ready for her tour. She was sure that would work out better than him taking the time to wait for her.

She sat on the edge of Mateo's bed and talked to both boys about the plans she'd made. "I'm marrying Bob tomorrow, so he's going to be your daddy, as you know. We'll move into his cabin this weekend. How do you like playing with Grandma?"

"We love her!" Antonio said.

Mateo nodded emphatically.

"And she's always nice to you?" Marta asked. As much as she liked the woman, Marta was worried that Beth was different when she wasn't around.

"Yes!" Mateo said.

"Wonderful." She leaned down and kissed Mateo on the cheek, tucking the covers around him, and then she went to Antonio and did the same thing. "I love you. Sleep well. When you wake up, go downstairs. If I'm not there, Grandma will be."

Antonio smiled. "Yes, Mama."

As she closed the door, Marta was still smiling. Being around this family...well, it had her smiling more than she had in years.

She walked over to the office from there, thinking about the conversation she still wanted to have with Beth, but that could wait. She had to see the house where she'd be living!

Finding Bob in his office, she saw he was on the phone again, so she sat in the chair opposite his desk. She couldn't believe it was just yesterday when she'd sat in the chair for the first time, praying that he would be willing to hire her.

When Bob finished his call—something about the wedding—he smiled. "Ready to go see the cabin?"

Marta nodded. "I'm excited."

"It's actually a little far from the main house. It's part of the wooded area where we do the Christmas village. April decorates the house and makes it look like it's just a prop, but it's really where I live." He held her hand as they walked, talking about everything around them. "That's the music room." He nodded to a building. "Dawn and April work their magic with the kids in there."

"Is April as good with music as Dawn?"

He smiled. "Not nearly. April's main interest has always been Christmas, and making it as amazing as possible. So instead of having a class of her own, she helps Dawn with the music classes. She's more crowd control than anything else. April can play a couple of instruments, and she sings all right, but I don't know anyone who can hold a candle to Dawn."

"I can't wait to hear Dawn sing," Marta said.

"She'll sing at our reception. She always does." He kept walking along a path, and she finally saw a house off in the distance, set apart from the majority of the activities on the ranch.

Marta's first impression of the house was that it wasn't a cabin like he'd said. It was more of a...well, a big house! It certainly wasn't as big as his parents' house, but why would he need something that big?

He led her to the front porch, where a swing hung from the roof. "The boys will love this swing," she said softly.

"When I designed this house, I tried to think of what I'd want for the family I would eventually have. Berry designed the kitchen to be a cook's dream, but I've never cooked in it. Not even once." He opened the door, which she noticed hadn't been locked, and let her step inside first. "It's not as neat as I'd like it to be, but I think it's all right."

The living room looked good to her, but there was a throw pillow on the floor. He stooped over and picked it up, and she couldn't help but admire his butt. "This is the living room, and there's the dining room," he said pointing to another room off the main one. "The kitchen is through here." There was a window that made it so whoever was cooking would be able to see the living room and know what was happening—even have a conversation—but the kitchen didn't feel like it was part of the living room.

Marta looked at the kitchen and smiled. "I've never cooked in a kitchen like this." Not only was there what looked to be a brand-new range to cook on, but there was also a wall oven and a built-in microwave. The fridge was a side by side, and she knew the boys would like to be able to get their own popsicles and other treats. The sink had three faucets, and she frowned at him. "Why three faucets?"

He smiled. "This was my idea. The faucet on the left is for washing dishes, and that sort of thing. The middle faucet is for drinking water. And the one on the right is for water that's just under boiling. It's just the right temp for tea or hot chocolate right out of the tap."

"I love that!" She grinned at him. "I'm going to enjoy cooking in here."

He led her to another room which was off the kitchen. "This is the mud room." There was a sink, washer dryer, and two doors. He opened the first door. "Half bath." It was just a potty and a sink. Opening the second door, he said, "Pantry."

Marta's jaw dropped. The pantry was huge, with shelves along three walls, and even some space under the shelves. She loved the idea of having enough food stored up to fill the pantry, because then she'd never again have to worry about where the boys' next meal would come from.

Currently a lone loaf of bread resided on one of the shelves. "You really don't eat at home!"

He grinned. "Why would I when I can eat every meal at my parents' house?"

"Are you going to want to eat every meal there after we marry?" she asked.

"I think that's up to you. When you don't feel like cooking, let Berry know there will be four more for supper. No big deal."

Marta smiled. "I couldn't even take the boys to McDonalds before, and now you're telling me we can have wonderful meals every day, and I still don't have to cook!" She shook her head. "You're spoiling me Bob Calendar."

"I think you deserve to be spoiled," he responded, dropping a quick kiss against her lips. "You're an amazing woman."

She shook her head, not understanding why he thought so much of her. She'd come to him penniless and living in her car. How was it he didn't think of her as a vagrant and tell her to get off his lawn?

He led her down the hall to a bedroom. "This is the master bedroom." He opened the door, and she saw a king-sized bed with shelves along the headboard. The shelves were filled with books on one side but there was nothing on the other. "I cleaned off the shelves on your side of the bed, so you can put your favorite books on it now."

Then he led her into the adjoining bathroom. There was a large bathtub with jets, and a separate shower. She could imagine soaking in it for hours on end. Of course, she'd have to give up sleep to do so, but it would be worth it on occasion.

There was even a chair in front of the mirror for her to sit in to put on makeup. "This is amazing, Bob. I can't wait!"

He smiled. "I'm glad. Now let's look at the other rooms. I'm going to have to borrow some beds from Mom's until the furniture I ordered last night is delivered."

Her eyes widened. "Why did you order furniture last night?"

"For the boys' room. I thought they'd like bunkbeds, and then I had to buy the whole set...It's a pirate theme, and the top bunk looks like a pirate ship. There's even a desk on one end of it. And stairs. There have to be stairs."

She laughed at the look on his face. "Is the bed for you or for the boys?"

"Well, I plan to sleep beside you...but I could play on the pirate ship too!"

"Now I know why you love my boys so much!"

Bob raised an eyebrow. "Yeah? Why?"

"Because you need playmates!"

He rubbed the back of his neck sheepishly. "Should I be ashamed of that?"

"I sure don't think so. It should be fun for you to have them around, and I know they're going to love having you to play with!"

He showed her the bedroom, and then he showed her another room across the hall. "I think this should be the nursery. You can decorate it any way you like."

She smiled, her hand touching the wall as she dreamed of a pink room with ruffles everywhere. But she couldn't do that. No, she'd make a Winnie the Pooh room for the baby, and if it happened to be a girl, they'd transition. "Do you want children of your own?" she asked.

He shrugged. "Honestly, it's up to you. You're the one who has to be pregnant and give birth to them. I'd be happy if we just had the three we already have, or if you wanted to pop out another ten, which is what my mother is after. Or we could adopt a handful, but then we'd have to add on to the house. Whatever makes you happy."

"Bob?"

"Yes?"

"Are you perfect?"

He chuckled. "Far from it. Ask any one of my sisters. I just...well, I love kids. I wouldn't ask you to do anything that could hurt you, like having a ton more kids, but I'm going to love the ones we have with everything inside me."

He walked to one last door. "I think I'm going to keep this as a guest room. Maybe your parents or siblings could visit."

She sighed. "They've never had an interest." She'd have to call her mom next week and tell her about the wedding, but it didn't matter if she knew in advance anyway. No one in her family had even gone to her first ceremony, and it was right there in town. Why would they travel across the country for her wedding?

"That's really sad. I hope you know; you're gaining a whole family who will love you unconditionally by marrying me, and not just a man who can't figure out how to cook to save his life."

"Well, I love your cabin. When you first called it a cabin, I thought it might just be a one room building for all of us to live in, and I wouldn't have complained one bit. But now...this place is beautiful."

He smiled. "I'm so glad you like it. Feel free to redecorate anything. I don't care."

As they walked back to the office, he talked about the move. "You can move a few things, or you can wait until after the wedding. I don't care. Mom is going to keep the boys tomorrow night. We get a whole night alone."

Marta bit her lip. "I'm not sure that's a good idea. Mateo has nightmares. His father was...cruel."

Bob frowned. The more he heard about the man she'd been married to, the more he wanted to hurt him. "Mom can handle it. I promise."

"They do love her already..." Marta nodded. "I'm going to ask the boys and let them decide if that's all right. I know you don't want them around for our wedding night, and I don't blame you for that, but I would like to know that they're where they feel comfortable."

He nodded. "That sounds reasonable. I wouldn't want them to be frightened without you."

She was so glad he understood. Leaving him at the office, she walked slowly back to the main house, wanting to talk to Beth. There was obviously more to his family's story than Bob knew, and she wanted to understand everything. Not that it mattered too terribly much. She was already falling for Bob, and she was going to marry him no matter what.

It seemed quick, but she already knew Bob better than she'd known Luis on their wedding night. No, this was the smartest thing she'd ever done, and her children were going to be much happier than they had been.

She walked through the camp seeing craft stations and groups of girls making jewelry. There were boys playing baseball, and a spot where boys—and it looked like one girl—were playing football. What a wonderful place Bob's family had created for children. And she would soon be part of it.

Chapter Eight

When Marta got back to the house, she found Beth in the living room with a crochet project this time. "The boys are still asleep?" she asked.

Beth nodded. "I haven't heard a peep out of them, but they played really hard this morning."

Marta sat down beside Beth, looking at the small disaster of cars and racetracks across the room. "Thank you so much for taking care of them for me. I appreciate it more than I can express."

Beth smiled. "They're delightful. I love how Antonio speaks for both of them, but Mateo is starting to speak as well. It's just...such a special relationship between the two of them."

Marta smiled. "It is. Antonio has always looked out for his little brother. And now they'll both look out for this one," she said, her hand going to her belly. It made her miss her own siblings when she thought about it, but they seemed to have lost all interest in her when she'd moved away.

"That's what's so special about siblings." Beth looked far away for a moment. "When Bert and I first got married, I knew I wanted thirteen children. He supported that and told me we'd make it happen. Then I couldn't get pregnant. It took me two years to get pregnant the first time, and I lost that baby."

Marta immediately closed her eyes. "I lost one too."

Beth sighed. "So many women have, but you're not really supposed to talk about miscarriages for whatever reason. But those lost babies...they're always in your heart." She shook her head. "When I had Bob, it was a difficult delivery. I had placenta previa and gestational diabetes. The doctor told me trying to have another baby would not be wise, and he wanted to immediately tie my tubes, so there was no chance of it."

"I'm so sorry!"

Beth smiled at her then. "I'm not. We decided to work on adopting when Bob was three, and I don't know where I came up with the brilliant idea to adopt three little ones at a time, but it worked. The months of the year came naturally with us being Calendars."

"My full name means Tuesday," Marta said softly.

"I knew you were one of us the moment I laid eyes on you."

"But how did you know to make a dress for me?" There was no doubt in Marta's mind that the dress Beth had made hadn't been for a nameless faceless stranger. It was made for *her*.

Beth smiled. "I can't tell you all my secrets now, can I?"

Marta sighed. "I guess not, but I sure would like to know."

"That's a story for another day." Beth's crochet hook resumed its former speed.

Marta decided not to argue because she knew it wouldn't do any good. She sat for a moment, and asked, "What else do I need to do for the reception?" she asked.

Beth gasped. "Oh, you haven't talked to Berry about food yet, have you?"

Marta shook her head. "Every time I see her, she's with a class."

After glancing at a clock on the wall, Beth called out, "Berry, can you come in here?"

Berry walked into the room, spotted Marta, and said, "Just a second." She hurried back out and came in with a notebook and pen. "I've come up with three ideas for food, and you just choose the one you prefer."

Marta smiled. "That will make it so much easier." Berry really was good at helping people plan events. Bob had mentioned that to her in passing, but Marta could see his sister really shined in that area.

"The idea I'm leaning toward is a taco bar. I would make chicken, ground beef, and steak tacos, and then everyone could choose between nachos, flour tortillas, or taco shells. We'd give the choice of two types of beans—black or refried pinto—and nacho cheese or grated cheddar. We can scoop them up and turn them into whatever anyone wants. We'll have lettuce, tomatoes, and sour cream available. And I could—"

"Yes," Marta said interrupting. "That sounds perfect to me."

"You don't even want to hear my other ideas?"

Marta shook her head. "No, that sounds like the perfect reception food for a Hispanic woman's wedding."

Berry grinned. "I was thinking the same thing. All right then. I'll get started prepping. Are you planning on inviting a lot of people?" she asked. "I already know who will come for Bob."

"I come to you with everyone in my life. My friends—the few I had—all quit speaking to me after Luis died. My family is in Texas, and they didn't go to my first wedding, which was in their town. It will be me and the boys."

Beth shook her head. "You, the boys, and the entire Calendar family. Remember, you're inheriting twelve new sisters."

Marta nodded, unsure how to respond to that. "Yes, but there will be no one giving me away."

Berry frowned. "Jack will do it."

"Who is Jack?"

"My husband, and he wants to be your father for the day. I'm texting him now."

"You can't expect him to just be willing to give me away." Marta frowned. Her own father hadn't cared enough to give her away. Why would a stranger?

"Sure, I can. I sleep with him." Berry smiled as she got a text back. "He said he'd be honored." Jumping to her feet, Berry said, "And we'll all be getting ready with you in the back of the church, just like we did with each other. You're really one of us now, Marta. And I'm off to the front of the house to gather my students for my next class."

With that, Berry was gone, and Marta sat in silence for a moment, wondering what on earth it all could mean. "I don't think I'm good enough for this family," Marta said softly.

"I know," Beth said, "but you are. Whether you married Bob or not, I've decided you're one of my daughters."

Marta wasn't sure what to say, but the boys came in like little tornadoes of energy taking her mind off trying to formulate a reply. Mateo went straight to Marta and climbed on her lap for a moment, snuggling close to her. She felt it was a good time to ask the boys if they wanted to stay with her or with their new grandma the next night.

"So, you boys know I'm going to marry Bob tomorrow. Do you want to stay with Grandma tomorrow night, or would you be scared?"

Antonio grinned. "We want to stay with Grandma. She already told us we could, and we're going to play and play, and eat cookies. We like cookies."

"I know you do!" Marta responded, smiling. "Do you want to stay with Grandma, Mateo?"

Mateo nodded, his eyes looking excited at the prospect. "You'll need to remember to go to her room if you get scared."

"Or he can climb in bed with me," Antonio suggested. "That's what he usually does."

There had been times Mateo had needed his mother in the night, and he'd tiptoed into his parents' room, afraid to be caught by his father. Her husband had felt that his boys needed a firm hand, and he was constantly angry with Marta for spoiling them.

"I guess that's all settled then, isn't it?" Marta asked.

"And the boys and I are going to have a packing party. We're going to get all their things packed up that night and ready to move."

Marta smiled, so thankful for this family and how they already loved her boys. Who could ask for more?

MARTA WAS AT THE CHURCH by two on Saturday afternoon for her four o' clock wedding. The Calendar sisters were gathered around her, and she had to admit if only to herself, that the bridesmaid dresses really were hideous. She didn't dare tell the sisters that though, or they would burn them *before* her wedding took place.

Beth wouldn't let her clean the cabins that morning for fear she'd be spotted by Bob, so she had skipped her day of work, but Jana told her as soon as she got there that they'd finished. "It was kind of fun to work together that way. We divided into four groups and the groups raced to see who could finish their assigned cabins first. My group won of course."

"Did not!" Sparky said. "My group won!"

Novel rolled her eyes. "We all won because the work is done, and we get to wear these hideous dresses as prizes." She held the dress out to both sides and spun in a circle, causing her sisters to laugh.

Julia, whom Marta had met late yesterday afternoon, offered to do her hair and makeup. "You need a haircut," Julia complained as she finished Marta's makeup and moved on to doing her hair. "I'll still make you look beautiful."

Berry clucked her tongue. "Like anything could make her not look beautiful. Her skin is amazing!"

Beth popped into the back room then and smiled. "Are you nervous?" she asked Marta.

Marta thought about it for a moment and shook her head. "I was really nervous the first time, but this time, it just feels right. Does that make sense?"

"It does." Beth sat down. "Don't worry about the boys. I have Bert and Bob playing dad and granddad. If you hear squeals, they'll be squeals of excitement. They've been reminded not to break anything."

Shaking her head, Marta laughed. "I guess squeals of excitement are a good thing. It means my boys are happy."

"*Our* boys are happy. Are you going to be nervous about them all night, or will you be okay with me watching them?" Beth asked.

"I'll be a little nervous of course, but I'll be fine. They chose to stay with you, which means they're comfortable. Just listen for Mateo. He has nightmares. Usually, he just climbs in bed with Antonio, and they're fine, but sometimes he will want to get in bed with me."

"I'll make sure to sleep in pajamas and not naked then."

As Marta watched, all twelve of Beth's daughters cringed. "TMI, Mom!" Novel protested.

"Well, if you want to know, Bert and I still have a very active love life, and—"

As one, her daughters yelled, "We don't want to know!"

Beth laughed, a hearty sound that filled the room with happiness.

Marta grinned. She loved this family a little more with every minute spent with them.

After a few more minutes, Julia declared Marta ready, and when she turned to look in the mirror, she laughed. "If it wasn't for my very pregnant belly, I'd look about sixteen."

"You have good bones," Julia said admiring her handiwork.

Berry slipped out the door then, and Marta knew she was checking the food. Brunhilda, who Marta had yet to meet because she'd been in Helena shopping with her sister, was supposed to be watching over it, but Berry had said Brunie couldn't always be trusted, and she just prayed she was speaking English for a change.

Marta wasn't sure what that meant, but she wouldn't complain. She was surrounded by people who liked her or at least pretended to, which was absolutely amazing, and she was about to marry the kindest man she'd ever met. Surely life was turning around for her.

Bert popped his head in the door, his eyes covered with one hand. "Everyone get out here. Let's get this wedding over with, and then we can have tacos."

Marta watched as all the sisters lined up in age order and left, Dawn with her hand on Novel's shoulder to help her see the way. Berry hurried past the room to take her place with the others.

Marta followed slowly, walking to the area at the back of the church where she couldn't be seen. There was a man standing there, smiling at her. "Marta?"

She nodded. "Yes, I'm Marta."

"Jack Larson, Berry's husband. I understand I'm your father today."

Marta laughed. "Hello, Dad."

"Hiya! You ready to get this show on the road?"

"I really am. I don't like people looking at me, but in a wedding dress, that's what's going to happen. Of course, I love the dress, so I can't complain too terribly much."

"No, you can't." He offered her his arm and the wedding march started playing, and she walked down the aisle, happy to have something to cling to.

"Thank you so much for doing this for me. I thought about asking Bob's dad, but that would have been weird."

Jack chuckled. "Nah. He's done it so many times now, it's second nature."

Marta grinned as he put her hand in Bob's. Bob's smile filled her heart so full, she worried she was going to explode.

Then the pastor started speaking. "Dearly beloved. We are here for the last time with this ridiculously large family to add yet another member to it. Bob Calendar, the oldest of all the Calendar children, has finally chosen a bride, and it doesn't look like they're marrying a minute too soon. No one told me about the baby on the way, but I'm a modern pastor, and I would have married them no matter what." He went on and on, but after that, Marta tuned him out because Bob was looking at her with a sweet look in his eyes, but he was obviously trying not to laugh at the same time. This pastor was a strange one.

When Pastor Dinkleheimler pronounced them husband and wife, Bob didn't hesitate. He put his hands on Marta's waist and pulled her to him, kissing her passionately.

He pulled away when the pastor cleared his throat. "I didn't say you could kiss the bride yet!" He looked at them for a moment. "Now, you may kiss your bride."

Bob didn't have to be told twice. He kissed her again, much to the amusement of everyone in the congregation watching them. Pastor Dinkleheimler had married all his sisters except October, who had eloped, and this was the first wedding where he hadn't licked his fingers and stuck them in the sky. Of course, this time he was wearing a face mask around his neck. Bob wasn't sure about the face masks, or why one would be around the man's neck, but he wasn't going to ask. He was married to Marta. All was right with the world.

Together, Bob and Marta stopped and each of them took one of the boys' hands, and they walked to the back of the church together. Mateo had cookies all over his borrowed suit, and Marta stopped to brush them off. "There. You look awfully handsome today, Mateo."

Antonio grinned. "You look pretty, Mama. I like your dress."

"Grandma made it for me," Marta said, spinning so the skirt flared out around her. Of course, that wasn't great for her pregnant stomach, and she stopped, holding it for a moment. "The nausea hits at some of the worst times."

Bob shook his head. "No more spinning then. Shall we go see what the reception hall looks like?"

"I'd love that."

"Oh, Berry made my favorite cake. I hope you don't mind not having a say."

She shook her head. "No, I chose the food."

"White chocolate raspberry. I may not share."

Laughing, she linked her arm with his and walked with him to the fellowship hall where the reception would be. He was going to keep her on her toes. That much was certain.

Chapter Nine

The fellowship hall was filled with people, many of them family, others who knew the family or were friends with Bob. Marta was surprised at the sheer number of people there, saying best wishes and how happy they were for her and Bob. It was strange.

The boys immediately pulled away from Marta, and when asked where they were going, Antonio answered for both. "Grandma!"

"I guess I should have known," Marta said to Bob. It was odd to her because the boys had never had the opportunity to bond with anyone but her, and here they were, in love with Bob's mother. It was good though. She was sure it would be better for them to know other people, but it was strange to see them form such a close bond so quickly.

Bob smiled. "She's like a pied piper for children."

"I see that!" Marta started walking toward her new in-laws, wanting to be with people she knew.

When they got to them, it seemed Beth was telling a story. "...had the two-year-olds for Sunday school, and Bob was part of the group. When I taught the lesson about God creating the heavens and the earth, the children misheard me. They thought Bob created the heavens and the earth. It took me weeks to explain it was God and not Bob. I'd go home thinking they understood that it wasn't Bob, and the next week when I asked who created the heavens and the earth, they'd all yell, 'Bob!' and point at Bob. I couldn't live in a world where Bob was the one who created everything." Beth shook her head. "And now he's grown up to be a good man, and I can't even complain about him a little."

The woman she was speaking to laughed, shaking her head as well. "I remember that. You were mortified and called me to see if I could give you advice about fixing it."

Beth nodded. "Marta, this is my aunt Griselda. She worked on the Cauldron Valley Ranch. Griselda, this is Marta, Bob's wife and the mother of these two lovely boys."

Griselda smiled at Marta. "It's so good to meet you. We all wondered if it was possible for Bob to ever meet a woman who would put up with his...perfection."

"He told me he's not perfect," Marta said, grinning at her husband.

Griselda groaned loudly. "Admitting he's not perfect just makes him seem...well, more perfect! I don't know how the man became so wonderful, but it is strange to me."

Marta looked at Bob, who was doing his best to ignore the entire conversation. He looked a bit embarrassed, and she had to wonder how he felt about the people who were always calling him perfect.

Instead of asking, she said quietly, "Let's go get our food." She looked at the boys. "Come with me, and I'll help you get your dinner."

Antonio shook his head. "Grandma is going to help us get food."

Beth smiled and waved her hand. "You two go be newlyweds and forget about the boys until tomorrow."

"I can't forget my boys!" Marta said, her eyes wide.

"Then know they are taken care of."

Bob smiled at her and nodded. "It's really okay. Let's go see what Berry came up with."

There were four people behind a long counter. The first—an older woman—said, *"Que' te traigo?"*

Marta smiled and explained what she wanted in the language of her parents. When her plate was filled, she said, *"Soy Marta. Y tu?"*

"Brunhilda."

"Oh! It's so nice to meet you. No one said you could speak Spanish fluently."

Brunhilda glared at Bob.

"I'll explain when we sit down," he said to Marta.

As soon as they were seated, Bob leaned forward. "Brunhilda speaks a different language every month. Sometimes it seems as if she's just spouting gibberish, but by the end of the month, Dawn can usually understand her. And Sparky has an app that translates her. I don't know why she does it because no one really understands or responds."

"It was smart of Sparky to get an app like that!"

Bob grinned shaking his head. "I said it wrong. Sparky *created* the app."

"Oh! She seemed really smart when I met her earlier."

"Trust me, she is."

"Truthfully, your sisters are just a bit overwhelming. Each of them seems to have something that they're so good at, no one else in the world could compare."

Bob laughed. "And you haven't even heard Dawn sing yet."

A short while later, all the tables were moved to one side, and the wedding guests gathered around for Bob and Marta's first dance together as a married couple...well, really their first dance together.

Dawn stepped up to the microphone with the help of Todd, and she removed it from the stand and held it instead. And as soon as she opened her mouth, Marta understood. Dawn was a truly gifted singer.

As Marta and Bob swayed back and forth to the music, and they looked into one another's eyes, she realized she already had stronger feelings for Bob than she ever had for Luis. She'd married Luis because her father told her to, and she was an obedient daughter. Marrying Bob hadn't really been a decision. It had felt like the most natural thing in the world to do. He made her feel alive for the first time in years.

After the dance, they cut the cake, and then to her surprise, Bob suggested she say goodnight to the boys. "We're not staying any longer?" she asked.

"If you want to, we can, but I was hoping for just as much time alone with my bride as possible while my mom has the boys."

She bit her lip. "Are you saying you don't want the boys around?" Luis had said that so many times it was hard for her to understand why anyone would care about her boys.

"I would never say that. Say goodnight, and we'll talk. All right?"

Marta nodded, going to her boys who were dancing and talking excitedly in the middle of the dancefloor. She realized they'd never really had an opportunity to dance before, and they were making the most of the situation.

Both boys hugged her, and Bob lifted them to get a kiss goodnight. "I can lift them!" she protested.

"You're not doing anything to risk our baby. You shouldn't be lifting," he said.

His words told her so much about him. He was referring to the child she carried as their baby.

After she hugged and kissed each boy, Bob did the same. "Be good for Grandma, and we'll see you right after church tomorrow. I love you both!"

To Marta's surprise, it wasn't Antonio who responded. It was Mateo. "I l...l...love you."

Marta couldn't help the tears that started streaking down her cheeks. Antonio frowned at her. "We love Bob!"

She smiled at her older son to let him know she approved of the love, but she couldn't seem to stop the tears. "I'm happy you love him," she said, but it was Mateo who really made her cry. He worked so hard to tell his new daddy he loved him, and Bob accepted it so readily. It didn't matter to him that Mateo stuttered. He really did care about her boys.

As they left the church and went out to his truck to head back to the ranch, he wrapped his arm around her. "You all right?"

She nodded. "I never pictured myself marrying again after the disaster that was my marriage with Luis, and here you are, loving my boys immediately. He never loved them. Not one bit."

Bob shook his head. "I wanted to take you straight home and ravish you, but I think we're going to have to talk first. I'd say you're breaking my heart, but my heart has nothing to do with it. It's other portions of my anatomy that are suffering."

"We can talk after we take care of your other portions..."

"No, I think we need to get this talk out of the way."

He drove to the ranch, not saying a whole lot. There was too much going on in his mind. Her first husband sounded like he was much worse than Bob had first thought, and he needed to know more. She couldn't give her heart to him as he so desperately craved until they'd talked about her past and exorcised all the demons in her mind.

He pulled up in front of the house, and walked around to open her truck door, picking her up and carrying her to the door. When he got there, he stopped. "So, I didn't think this out very well. I don't suppose you'd open the door for me, would you?"

Marta couldn't help but laugh. This man brought out all the emotions from her, and she had no complaints. He was special, and that's all there was to it. She turned the knob for him, and he carried her to the couch, and set her down there.

"Mom and Aunt Griselda carried all your things from Mom's house to my room here while you were at the church. We'll have to move the boys' things tomorrow, but your things are here."

"I should change then. I don't want to mess up this dress."

Bob held up a hand. "It's my job to take that dress off you, and if I do it now, there's no way we'll have this talk. Sit first and undress later."

"Well, when you put it that way..." She slid closer to him on the couch, wanting to be intimate with him. Talking was a waste of their alone time.

Bob shook his head. "You have no idea how much I want to just carry you off and have my way with you, but...I want to hear about your marriage to Luis. You said you thought he was handsome, and he talked to your father right after graduation, and your father said you should marry him..."

She closed her eyes for a moment and nodded. This was not the time she wanted to have this discussion. "That's all true."

"Did you love Luis?"

"Not particularly. In my family, marriage is what's expected of a young woman. Sure, she can go to school, but she's there to find a man to marry her and give her babies." Marta was embarrassed to admit all this, but she didn't know what else she could do but talk to him about the truth. She wasn't sure if it was true of all of the Mexican culture, but she knew it was true of her family. "When he asked Papa if he could marry me, Papa told me I *must* marry him. There was no choice in the matter for me. I did what I was told, and I married him three days later."

"Why didn't you wait and have a wedding?" Bob asked, confused.

"Papa told me I couldn't. As the oldest, it was my duty to marry quickly so I wouldn't be a burden on the family for any longer than necessary. So, I married him, and that was that."

"And he was your...first?"

Marta nodded. "He was. Before you, I had never even been kissed by another man."

"And he was a good husband?"

She shrugged. "It depends on what you mean by good. For the time we lived in Texas, he would come home after work, and it seemed like it was working out well between us. Then he said he could make more at a ranch in Montana, and like an obedient bride, I followed him here. I found out I was pregnant the following month. As soon as I was pregnant, I think he considered his job with me done. He spent more and more time out of the apartment we shared. He would come home in time to sleep and that was all. If he was awake when the boys were, he was angry with me for not having them asleep. He was terrible with Mateo's stammer. He yelled at him all the time about it until Mateo quit speaking around anyone but me and Antonio, and then it was rare." She took a deep breath. "I don't think I would have lasted with him for much longer, but I don't believe in divorce, so my heart was torn. I didn't want him around the boys, and I didn't want to be his wife, but…I keep my promises."

Bob nodded. "Did you ever love Luis?"

Marta closed her eyes and shook her head. "No, I never did. But I was a good, dutiful wife. The money I made at the hotel paid for our bills, and anything Luis made was put into a different account, and I don't know what he did with it. He bought me a minivan, and I liked it, but I took it back to the bank. I have no idea how it was paid for, and I won't keep anything that came from his crimes."

"I'm not the kind of man your husband was. I will be involved in any decisions regarding our children, and I will spend just as much time with them as I can. You can work or not work. My house was built for me, and I paid for it as I went along. There are no big bills to pay, and we can easily live on my income." He took a deep breath. "Our marriage will be much different."

"I hope so. You…well, everything about you makes me feel like we belong together, and we should spend our lives together. I am happy you're not like Luis. He was cruel to the boys. He was never physically abusive with me, but he was uncaring. I sometimes wonder if he married me so he could stay in this country. He was here on a green card when I met him."

"Well, I think you are too special to be in a relationship like that. I fell in love with you the moment you looked at me so defiantly and offered me your license plate number for an address. I hope you don't mind love in a marriage, because I plan on making you feel like it's a crime for a man *not* to love you."

Chapter Ten

"Wait...are you saying you asked me to marry you because you love me?" Marta couldn't believe Bob's words. How could he love her when he barely knew her? But how could she know marriage to him would be wonderful when she'd just lived through a marriage of indifference?

He nodded. "How could I not fall in love with you? I couldn't fall for anyone at all until Dawn was settled because I was sure it was going to be the two of us, both unmarried, holding down the ranch. But after she married...well, that's when God brought you into my path, and I knew that you were the right woman. I'd already fallen for your boys."

Marta wanted to say the words back to him. She wanted to make him smile...but she wasn't sure, and she couldn't tell him she loved him and take it back in a month when she was sure. No, it would be better to wait...to see how she felt before she said the words, and she'd have to pray he wouldn't hate her for it.

"I'm...I'm not ready to say that yet."

Bob gripped both of her hands in his. "With what you've been through it would be almost impossible for you to say it so soon. I pray that one day you'll be able to say you love me as well, but if it doesn't come, it doesn't. I understand."

At his words, Marta lurched into him and held on for dear life. This man, this wonderful special practically perfect man, he even understood why she couldn't love him yet. Never again would she feel alone because Bob was with her.

Bob held her close, burying his face in her hair. After a moment, he pulled away and cupped her face in his hands, lowering his mouth to hers. This kiss was so much more than the others they'd shared. This kiss was passionate and held all the desire he had for her.

She returned the kiss with everything inside her, her hands coming up to slide his suit jacket off his shoulders, and then her hands went to work on his tie. When she couldn't figure it out, she pulled back and looked up at him questioningly.

He grinned. "It's a clip on. I can't tie a tie to save my life!"

With that, Marta laughed. "I think I can live with a flaw that big..."

He got to his feet and held a hand down for her. When she put her hand in it, he pulled her into the bedroom. "Now, I'm getting this dress off you. It's our wedding night!"

Marta turned her back to him, so he could unzip the dress. "I'm pregnant, so don't expect the body under this dress to be perfect..."

"The body is swollen with our child. How could I complain about how you look when it's my baby inside you?"

She tilted her head to one side as she turned to face him, holding the bodice of the dress in place. "Do you really consider this baby your own?"

He nodded. "Of course, I do. I can't wait to hold him or her in my arms. Are you sure we can't find out the gender?" he asked.

"We can't. I just...no, we will wait and know when the midwife tells us that the baby is a boy or a girl. That's how it should be."

"All right. If that's what you want, then that's how we'll handle it." He reached for her, pulling the dress from her and watching as it fell to the floor. She stood before him in just a white slip as well as her other undergarments, and he could see the gentle swelling of her stomach. His hands rested against her belly. "Hello in there! I'm your daddy, and I can't wait to meet you!"

Marta laughed. "You're a silly Bob."

"We'd better slow down here...you're finding out all my flaws in one night. I'm not so sure that's a good idea..."

"Do you always talk when you make love?" she asked.

He shrugged. "I don't know. I've never done this before."

She gaped at him for a moment. "You haven't?"

"No. How could I? Before this week you weren't in my life." He leaned down for another kiss, and she clung to him, wanting this experience to be perfect for him and wishing she could not be pregnant just for the next hour.

They slowly undressed each other, kissing the entire while. When he pushed her onto her back on the bed, she reached up and stroked his shoulders. Already he'd spent more time with her than Luis had in the past three years. Bob was so different than anyone she had ever met, and she felt blessed to be his wife.

When he covered her body with his, and joined them in the primal dance of lovers, she knew without a doubt that she was his. He'd sealed their bodies together, and that's what she needed at that moment.

As she lay with her head on his shoulder, her hand stroking his chest, she sighed contentedly. "We should do that often," she said.

He chuckled. "I'm not opposed to that idea at all. In fact...it may make me happier than anything ever has."

"I'm glad you were the one to come along and turn my life upside down. It's weird to be married to a man who is full of perfections, but..."

Bob groaned. "Stop listening to the Bob-praganda. I'm not perfect in any way shape or form. Remember what my mom said about living in a world where I was the creator?"

"I loved that story," she said, grinning at him. "You are pretty special. Thank you."

He frowned at her thanks. "Don't thank me. I do what I do out of love." He hoped she hadn't married him out of gratitude. Knowing that would break his heart. He only needed one thing from her, and that was love. Gratitude is not what he wanted. Ever.

THE FOLLOWING DAY WAS busy with getting the boys moved to the new house. Antonio was excited to sleep in a room with no furniture. "Do we *have* to get beds, Daddy?"

Bob laughed. "Your beds have been ordered and will be here in a week, but you're getting bunk beds! Won't that be exciting?"

Antonio shrugged, looking at the empty floor with the sleeping bags and pillows on it. "I guess..."

Mateo nudged his brother. "B...b...bunk beds!"

"They'll be fun, but I get the *top* bunk!" Antonio finally agreed.

Berry had sent home some of lunch so Marta wouldn't have to cook anything for supper, and she had been thrilled. As she hung the boys' things and put their clothes on the shelf in the closet, Bob played with the boys in the living room. He hadn't been willing to wait for toys and instead they'd made an emergency trip to Helena and the nearest Walmart so the boys would have a good supply of toys to play with.

Marta listened to them play and she couldn't help smiling. Bob really was good with them.

After supper, they bathed the boys together and put them into their "beds." Bob told them a story that went along with the new trains and tracks he'd purchased that were now stretched all through his living room. As Marta listened, she couldn't help but smile, watching the man tell her children an animated story with different voices and wide gestures.

After they left the room, she looked at Bob and said, "You have no idea how thankful I am that you love my boys."

Bob couldn't help but frown. "I'm not perfect, and I really don't want your gratitude."

"You don't?"

"No! I'm doing what I want to do. I married the woman I love, and I enjoy spending time with her boys, whom I also love!" He shook his head. "You don't need to run around thanking me all the time for doing things with the people I love!"

Marta blinked a few times, but nodded, walking into the kitchen to do the dishes. She didn't expect him to follow. Anytime Luis had spoken to her that way, she'd had to hide from him for fear he would take his anger out on the boys.

In the kitchen, she wondered if she'd just ruined her marriage by being thankful. Surely, if she could stop herself from thanking him every ten minutes, he would be able to forgive her. At least she hoped he would.

Bob walked into the kitchen and watched her load the dishwasher. "I'm sorry, I snapped at you. I didn't mean to. When you thank me, it makes me feel like you married me because you wanted a way out of your situation, and I hate to think that's the only reason you married me."

Marta shook her head, seeing that he was no longer angry, and just looked sad. She put the dish she was holding into the dishwasher, and hurried toward him, getting water on him as she threw her arms around him. "I'm so sorry I made you feel that way. I married you for a lot of reasons, but the biggest one was that I was so attracted to you. Every time I looked at you, I wondered what you'd look like with a little less clothing on."

"Really?" he asked, gazing down into her face. "You mean it?"

"Yes, my lust got the better of me, and so I married you. I hope you don't think less of me."

He laughed. "How could I? I like that you're lusting after me."

She went back to the dishes, and he thought about offering to help, but she was efficient, and he was sure he would just slow her down. Besides, he hated doing the dishes. When she finished, she started the machine and then looked at him. "I'll always lust after you Bob."

He chuckled. "That's almost as good as love." Taking her hand, he led her off to the bedroom, saying a silent prayer that love would come soon.

BY THE TIME THEY'D been married a full week, Marta knew exactly how she felt. She'd seen Bob at his worst when he'd been angry with her the day after they married. He sometimes got annoyed with her, but he always told her what was wrong, and they worked through it easily. He was just a good, even-tempered man for the most part.

And she loved him.

It hit her over the head how she felt about him when he helped her clean each of the cabins after the campers moved out. "You don't need to help me," she said for the umpteenth time. "I get paid to clean the cabins."

He shrugged. "I can't let you do so much when you're carrying my baby."

Surprisingly, it wasn't the fact that he helped her clean that made her realize she loved him. It was his constant talk about the baby coming, and *their* boys. He was looking into a speech therapist for Mateo, and he kept insisting that they needed to get him help before he started school. He didn't want their son to be teased.

She dropped the cloth she was using to clean the mirrors over the sink where there were toothpaste splatters and walked to him, throwing her arms around him. "I love you, Bob Calendar!"

He pulled away, looking into her eyes. "I love you too, Marta Calendar." He held her close for a moment, and then asked, "Are you sure?"

"I am positive. You're not perfect, and I've found some of your flaws. But you *are* perfect for me." She clung to him for a moment, and then she walked back and picked up the cloth she'd been using.

Bob stood there with a silly grin on his face for a minute before he resumed mopping the floors. Life was about as good as it could possibly get. Marta and the boys completed him, and he knew the baby she carried would be exactly what he needed to be happy. Life was so good with Marta by his side.

Epilogue

In the birthing suite of the Cauldron Valley Midwifery Clinic, Bob knelt on the floor beside Marta's bed, their hands twined together. Bob was half-praying and half supporting as Marta squeezed his hand, her fingernails drawing blood. "You're doing great," the midwife said. "Another push or two, and we will be there!"

Wanting to whimper and say she just couldn't do it, Marta looked over at Bob who smiled and nodded.

"You've got this. I can't wait to see her." He'd taken to calling the baby her, because she was convinced it was another boy, and she kept calling it him. It was his little way to be persnickety.

Seconds later, the next contraction hit, and Marta pushed with everything she had. "I see the head! You can do it, Marta!"

And then the slippery baby was in the midwife's hands, and she carefully cleared out the mouth and nose. "It's a girl."

Marta lay back against the headboard, her eyes glued to the baby. They were the words she'd so desperately wanted to hear, but... "Are you sure?"

The midwife laughed softly. "I'm positive. Ten fingers, ten toes, and a perfect set of lungs," she said over the cries of the baby, who wasn't too pleased with leaving her safe, warm home of the past nine months. "Bob, will you hold her while I cut the cord and get her mama cleaned up a little?"

Bob walked to the child, mesmerized by the cries coming out of the tiny body. He took her and his heart grew ten sizes. "You're perfect. Your brothers and I are going to watch over you and no boy is going to get to touch you until you're at least fifty-three." Never in his life had he dreamed that he would feel so much, holding a newborn baby.

When the midwife turned to him to take the baby back so she could be weighed, he didn't want to let her go. This was his child—his daughter—and he would protect her with his life.

As soon as he gave the baby to Carol, midwife-extraordinaire, he looked at Marta, who had been watching him with the baby. Until that moment, he hadn't realized his face was covered in tears.

He walked to his wife and knelt on the floor beside her again, promising himself that if they had more children, he would have kneepads. "She's the most beautiful thing I've ever seen in my life, and I'm sorry, but she's even prettier than you are."

Marta laughed. "I can't wait to hold her."

"It's the most wonderful experience in the world. I know because I got to hold her already."

She stroked the side of Bob's face, her love for him overflowing. "You were the best birth coach ever. Thank you for riding beside me in the roller coaster of life."

"Me? I couldn't do any of this without you." He kissed her softly and turned as the midwife gave the baby to Marta.

Marta stared down at the baby, and then looked at Bob. "What are we going to call her?" she asked. They hadn't talked about names really because they wanted to see her and come up with ideas while looking at the baby's face.

"How would you feel about calling her Elizabeth? After my mother."

"I like that," she said. "Elizabeth Ana."

He smiled. "Perfect. Elizabeth Ana Calendar. The very newest Calendar girl."

The boys would be officially adopted by Bob soon, and they would all be Calendars. "I don't want anyone to see her until Christmas. Can we wait?"

Bob nodded. "We'll tell them we need a few days alone to bond with the baby."

"And the boys?"

"The boys need to bond too," he said, smiling.

"Good. I want you to fetch them from your mother's house when we get home. The boys need to meet their sister."

Bob glanced at the time on his phone. "It's five in the morning. Is it okay if we wait until they wake up?"

She laughed. "I guess so."

MARTA COVERED THE BABY carrier in a blanket, knowing full well her child would be cold on the short walk to the main house. She was wearing her diaper, a onesie, a one piece sweat suit, mittens, hat, and now the quilt Beth had made for her.

Bob was getting the boys ready, and they came out of their room all bundled up to walk the short distance through the snow. "Are you sure you feel up to walking?" Bob asked. "I can drive you over."

Marta shook her head. "As long as the baby is warm enough, and I'm sure she is, we'll be fine."

They walked along a sidewalk that had candy canes on each side and had been shoveled by Bob himself the night before so he knew that it would be all right for them to walk to his parents' house on Christmas morning.

The house was lit up from afar, and Bob knew that April was loving having her own place because that was even more decorating she could do.

When they reached the house, Bob opened the door, and the boys walked in. "Merry Christmas!" Antonio shouted.

"Happy day!" Mateo said. His stuttering was getting better, but Christmas was still a hard word for him.

Beth came hurrying from the living room, peering at the baby. "Marta, I'm so happy you're here! I couldn't get Bob to even tell me if the baby was a boy or girl, so I'm waiting on pins and needles here."

Marta smiled. "You could have told her that." She shook her head at him, taking the quilt off the top of the carrier, and unbuckling the baby to take her out and hand her to her grandmother to hold. "Meet your new granddaughter. We named her Elizabeth Ana."

Beth stared down at the sleeping baby, tears streaming. "You named her after me?"

"Of course, we did!" Marta said. "I want her to be just like you, and what better way than starting her out with your name?"

Bert came down the stairs and smiled. "I thought I heard some noisy children!" He peered at the baby his wife was holding. "Boy or girl? Beth's been driving me crazy not knowing."

Bob smiled. "Dad, meet Elizabeth Ana."

The grin on his father's face made Bob prouder than he'd ever been. "She's beautiful, and she has a beautiful name to match," Bert finally said. "I think I need a turn holding her."

They went into the living room. "Berry's going to be here in fifteen, and she's bringing breakfast."

"I'm surprised she didn't just make it here," Bob said. "I hope it doesn't get cold."

"Don't be a pain, Bobert!" Beth said.

They heard footsteps and looked up as Dawn and Todd joined them in the living room. "So?" Dawn asked. "Boy or girl?"

"Elizabeth Ana," Bob said.

"She'd better be a girl then!" Todd said.

After a laugh, more of the Calendars came in. Jana and Brandon were next, along with Aubrey and Chad. Aubrey hurried to her grandmother, hugging her, while Jana sat down, taking Chad out of his carrier. "Grandma, guess what I got for Christmas!"

Beth smiled, knowing what her granddaughter had gotten, but feigning surprise. "What did you get?"

"I got lots of things, but I got what I wanted most! I'm adopted!"

Beth hugged the child. "Oh, that's wonderful! You're my granddaughter now!"

Aubrey laughed. "I always was!"

"That's very true."

Clint and October came in with Lacey, and Lacey carried a large package. They weren't exchanging gifts except for grandparents to grandchildren that day, so Bob asked what it was. "I made something for Grandma," Lacey said, looking a little embarrassed.

"Thank you, Lacey!" Beth said, standing to hug her teenage granddaughter.

"I hope you like it."

"I'm sure I will. Do you want me to open it now, or wait til later?"

"Oh, wait til later. Much later!"

October laughed, shaking her head. "You're going to love it, Mom. Lacey and I designed it together, but she did all the work on it herself."

Berry arrived then, following Jack in. "I've got four huge breakfast casseroles in the truck, and I'd better get some help!" she said. "And I have a present for you, Mom."

As Bob and Clint went out to help with the food, Jack took Berry's hand. Novel and Tyler came in with the girls right behind them. Berry cleared her throat, a shy grin on her face. "Mom, we're expecting, and we found out Friday that it's twins."

"Twins?" Mom asked. "I get to be the grandmother of twins!"

Novel groaned. "You stole my thunder, Berry! I was just about to announce I'm having a baby, but I'm only having one. You always have to upstage me!"

"Sorry, not sorry," Berry said, hugging her sister. "We're having babies!"

"Of course, you are." Mom got in on the hugging. "Remember, I still expect thirteen from each of you."

Marta groaned. "As someone who gave birth four days ago, I'm going to say I'm not sure I can do ten more." She knew immediately that her three counted, whether they were blood related to Beth or not.

When Sparky and Jax walked in, it was to a large group of people hugging. "Are we hugging or eating?" Sparky asked.

"How's the ghost-busting going?" Novel asked.

"I have a case! Hopefully, it will be more real spectral activity than I've found so far, but I'm determined that this time, it's a real ghost!" Sparky looked excited.

Jax smiled, his arm around his wife. He always looked like he half-worshipped his little bride.

Cord carried in the baby while Val brought up the rear with the diaper bag. "Mattie is so fussy this morning. She only wants her daddy, and she doesn't want anyone else to look at her." Val collapsed on the couch beside Marta. "Hey! How are you feeling? Where's the baby?"

Marta pointed to Bert, who was sitting there, staring down into the baby's face. "Elizabeth Ana," she said, loud enough for everyone to hear.

"Well, we know who gets the child-bearing brownie points!" Novel said.

Marta laughed.

"Who are we still missing?" Beth asked, looking around her.

"Marci and Tom, April and Cole, May and Adam, Junie and Poll, Julia, Brent and the boys. They're taking forever," Novel complained. "I'm pregnant and hungry."

No one dared comment that it was the second time she'd mentioned she was pregnant.

"Everyone is supposed to be here at ten, and it's only nine-forty-five," Beth said. "You're going to have to hold your horses."

"Breakfast is getting cold!" October complained.

"No, I have everything in quilted holders so they'll stay hot. Stop worrying," Berry said.

April and Cole came in then with April wearing a Christmas hat and Cole being a reluctant elf with ears and everything. "Merry Christmas!"

"Merry Christmas!" Beth responded. "You must have gone for a walk in the snow this morning. You have your Christmas glow written all over your face."

"That would be a pregnancy glow," April said, grinning.

Novel looked at April. "Don't expect it to be special. Berry just said she's having twins, completely eclipsing yours and my pregnancy."

April laughed, hugging Novel. "We're having babies!" Marta could tell April wasn't at all bothered that Berry was having twins.

Marci and Tom came in next. Marci's baby bump wasn't big, but she was definitely showing. "Merry Christmas everyone." Tom had his arm around Marci. He'd been watching her like a hawk since she'd gotten pregnant. It was as if he expected her to spontaneously combust any moment.

Beth's phone rang and she picked it up quickly. "Adam had an emergency at the hospital, but he just got home. He's showering the blood off him, and they'll be here."

"Good thing they're close," Novel grumbled.

Beth rolled her eyes. "Run in the kitchen and get yourself some crackers to tide you over."

"You don't have to tell me twice," Novel said, hurrying into the kitchen with her youngest daughter, Jessica, following close behind her.

Julia, Brent, and the boys came in then, all of them laughing about something. Julia's older son, Greg, carrying what was obviously a canvas, wrapped up. "I painted something for you, Grandma!"

Beth clapped excitedly. "I want to see it."

Andy hurried in and climbed on Beth's lap. "I've already seen it, but it's cool. Not as cool as playing cars with Uncle Bob, Antonio, and Mateo, but still cool."

"Do you want to unwrap it?" Greg asked.

Beth got to her feet and unwrapped the painting, her hand going over her mouth. It was a portrait of Beth, holding a baby Julia. He'd asked to borrow the picture months before. "It's beautiful. Thank you, Greg!"

"I'm not as good as Mom is yet, but I'm trying."

"You're much better than Mom was at your age," Julie told him, and it sounded like she'd reminded him of the same thing many times.

Junie and Poll came in next, and Junie smiled at everyone. "Merry Christmas!"

"Merry Christmas!" April said back. "Novel is in the kitchen pigging out because she's sure she's going to die if she has to wait another minute."

Novel came into the room from the kitchen, her mouth full. "I'm pregnant!" she protested, but it sounded more like, "'m egmum."

"She's pregnant," Berry translated, not mentioning her own pregnancy.

Junie smiled and hugged Novel. "Congratulations!"

Novel smiled. "Thank you. We're thrilled! When can we expect an announcement from you and Poll?"

"Poll rolled his eyes as he stepped up behind Junie and rested his chin on her shoulder. "According to my wife's five-year-plan, we're allowed to start considering children in eighteen months."

There was another round of laughter, and Val called out, "I thought you learned life doesn't always go as planned, Junie?"

"Yes," their mother agreed with a smile. "Sometimes it's better."

Together the sisters and Mom worked to set the table, Marta jumping up to help. "Where's Brunie?" Marta asked.

"Oh, they'll be along in a minute," Mom said.

By the time the table was set, and more chairs were pulled around to seat the ever-growing family, Brunie and Melvin and May and Adam had made it. "Sorry we're late," Adam said. "I'm on call this weekend, and there was a bad wreck. No one's dead, but there was *so much* blood."

May nodded. "I've never seen so much blood! I think he wore at least six pints home from the hospital."

Everyone sat, and Bert said a prayer over the meal, thanking God for another safe delivery of a grandbaby.

The table was full of talk and laughter, everyone excited that it was finally Christmas, but most especially April. It got to the point Marta could barely hear the boys as they talked to her, and they sat on either side of her.

Finally, a loud voice Marta had never heard said, "Would someone pass the orange juice please?"

All the talk at the table stopped, and everyone turned to stare at Melvin. "You talk?" Bob finally said to break the silence.

Melvin shrugged. "Always have." And he went back to eating as if he hadn't just changed the way everyone at the table would look at him forever.

April stood up and spread her arms wide. "It's a Christmas miracle!"

Melvin joined in the laughter. As everyone finished their breakfast, Marta thought about how thankful she was for Bob and this wonderful family she could now call her own.

Keep watching Kirsten and Caroline to see what they come up with next! There will be an announcement of their next series together around mid-September. For now, they're taking the summer off from writing together to concentrate on their families and their other books!

Caroline and I have loved writing this series together and hope to write lots more as a team. We laugh and get silly together at least once a month through video chats, so we can plan these for you! Please keep following us!

To get notifications, you can follow us on BookBub or join our email newsletters to receive more information on what we're doing. Follow us on Facebook or Instagram.

Thank you for supporting us!

Don't miss out!

Visit the website below and you can sign up to receive emails whenever Kirsten Osbourne publishes a new book. There's no charge and no obligation.

https://books2read.com/r/B-A-VSFD-GSGQB

BOOKS 2 READ

Connecting independent readers to independent writers.